WATCHER FRO

* * * * * * * * * *

JOHN WILSON

CHRISTIAN FOCUS PUBLICATIONS

To
John and Allison Sharp
not forgetting
Andrew, Ruth and John.
A family who are 'People of the Prince'.

©1991 John Wilson
ISBN 1 871676 72 X

Published by
Christian Focus Publications Ltd.
Geanies House, Fearn, Ross-shire,
IV20 1TW, Scotland, Great Britain.

Cover design by Seoris N. McGillivray

Printed in Great Britain

CONTENTS

Page

Introduction

I have no intention of starting any sort of extra-terrestrial cult, so I will not reveal how I came into possession of these reports. But I should admit that I do not know if these messages are intended for another planet, galaxy or dimension. All I do know is that reports are being sent from Shamar to Pzylon - whoever they are.

These reports show that we are being watched and our behaviour and lifestyle are being observed. The reports speak for themselves and I make no judgment on them. I leave the reader to judge their truth and value. Most of them are general observations on various aspects of our daily life and they differ in length and style. Some give detailed accounts of individuals and events while others make sweeping generalizations.

I find Shamar, the observer, a fascinating character. Although we have never met and I only know him through his reports, I feel I know him quite well. One thing that does come through all his writings is his sense of compassion; he seems to have a great love and pity for us.

Allied to this compassion is a bewilderment which, at times, seems to plunge him into utter despair. He struggles to understand the human condition but finds it almost beyond his capacity. In this, rather to my surprise, I find myself pitying him. He certainly did not enjoy his stay among us. The brief references to his own homeland make it easy for me to understand his homesickness.

There is one aspect of these reports which will, I suspect, surprise many. At times they seem to be religious, though not in any narrow sense. Shamar often refers to the 'Creator', a word not often used in contemporary discussions. It is clear that he believes that the world, the universe, and all things that exist, were actually created by God. Then, perhaps as a logical extension of this, he writes about 'creation' rather than our more familiar word 'nature'.

Some may find him equally old-fashioned in his observations on the Bible, Jesus, the Church and the Christian Faith. But, in spite of these comments, I would not say that these are simply religious reports. They are really impressions of our world by one particular observer from his own viewpoint.

Personally, I found these reports stimulating and, at times, challenging. It can be illuminating, and painful, to see ourselves as others see us.

I have resisted the temptation to edit or alter these reports in any way. I have retained even his occasional clumsy phrase, allowing him, in his own words, to 'wander around all sorts of subjects and events'. I believe it is better if they are read as originally written by Shamar, an obviously compassionate and bewildered observer. So I have left them, faults and all.

Shamar, the observer, seems to have a loving relationship to Pzylon to whom he reports. But at times irritation towards Pzylon and himself creeps in. It would be fascinating to be able to read the replies to these reports but all we have are the hints and asides which Shamar makes. Apparently, at times, he is accused of 'wordy wanderings' and 'wayward reporting' but, although ever ready to make apologies, Shamar is equally quick to give reasons and excuses. But I feel they are joined by a loving bond and no offence is meant or taken in their criticisms of each other.

Finally, I should say that each report title is my own invention and is based on the subject matter of the report. It will be obvious that Shamar's fondness for alliteration has influenced me in these report headings. This is not the only influence he has had on me.

Through these reports I have seen the world, and myself, through fresh, indeed innocent, eyes. It has been a revelation. They have made me more aware of the glory and the horror that surround me and all human-kind and have raised many questions to my mind. They even point to answers. I am glad I have read them. I can only send them out so that others may find, like me, that they are worth reading.

Beautiful but Blemished

Shamar to Pzylon: Earth Report 1

Greetings from a heart which is already heavy with the ache of homesickness. How I long to be back with you! Although I have only just arrived in this place I find myself painfully pining for the tranquility of my own homeland.

Earth is truly a place of glory and horror. I am so confused that I find it almost impossible to quieten my mind and compose my thoughts to compile this first report from this strange planet. A whirl of contradictory sensations overwhelm me and I have experienced a sense of awe shot through with agony. It is all so very strange.

My preliminary observations confirm previous reports that these human creatures have indeed a beautiful world in which to live. There is glory all around. There are hills and valleys, shining seas and sparkling rivers. There are petalled flowers in an endless variety of colours, trees in an astonishing range of shades and shapes, and almost everywhere there seems to be soft, green grass to carpet the hard earth. The sun is a glory by day with the moon and stars a shining comfort for the blackness of night. Beauty is here in abundance for those with eyes to see. Our great Creator has clearly done a beautiful thing here.

This planet is teeming with life in many forms. With my own eyes I have seen a bewildering variety of birds - winged, feathered creatures which soar and beautify the air. I have seen many different kinds of mammals which roam this Earth and innumerable species of swarming creatures in the oceans, seas and rivers of this place. The Creator must have had fun making such weird and wonderful inhabitants for this planet. There is a delightful sort of playfulness in having such a varied selection of strange creatures living together in one place.

This is indeed a place of grandeur and beauty but, tragically, it is also a place of horror. The beauty is blemished and all things seem flawed or cursed.

If untended the flowers are choked by weeds and in the animal realm the strong survive by preying on the weak. It is as if all things are out of harmony and the balance of creation is kept by terror. Most horrible of all, these living creatures are subject while they exist to disease and decay and finally everything - everything dies! It is a sad and pitiful reality. I am forced to wonder if this is a planet of glory shot through with pain, or a place of pain invaded by glory. Perhaps, in some strange way, both ideas are true. But I do not like it here. Indeed, I find myself wondering if the Creator has left this planet to its own sickness or, even more unthinkable, has left the Evil One to reign. Such things cannot be. Those thoughts must come from the confusion of my own mind.

But I have not mentioned the human creatures of this place! What can I say about man, a mammal also but the apex of all created creatures here?

He is like a god - intelligent, wide in his understanding, endowed with gifts beyond number - truly a creature of great ability and sensitivity. Earthlings stand high above all animals and the difference is not of size or degree but of kind. Each is a living soul. Such noble creatures bring to me feelings akin to awe. But that awe is tinged with despair. They are endowed with such power and so many gifts but they choose to abuse these continually. It is a tragic contradiction.

This contradiction is entirely confusing to me, a humble observer. The human creatures are capable of tender love yet can be viciously cruel. They can love and rape. Generosity and greed can be found in the same breast. They have an innate desire for the truth but can tell deliberate lies with no sense of shame. Although made with rational minds they often allow themselves to be governed by naked emotions. Indeed, many of them have the habit of depressing their rational and critical faculties by alcohol and other drugs. It is all so very strange and completely beyond my understanding.

In this sector of this strange planet, which from their perspective they call the 'West', these human creatures kill their unborn young when it is considered convenient. The medical term for this extermination of life is 'abortion'. What can I say about creatures who deliberately kill their own young? Words fail me! Ironically, it is considered uncivilised to execute those guilty of murder. They have compasssion for those who kill the old but no pity for unborn babies. Is that not most strange?

However, they are proud of being 'civilised' and consider themselves to belong to an advanced and compassionate age. In fact, they have had many wars to save 'civilisation' and these have been fought with a fury unworthy of any civilised planet.

Earthlings seem to have a love-hate relationship with war. Their children play with imitation weapons while the nations spend vast sums of money perfecting means of mass killings. It seems to be a planet of fear. Nations have great armies and armaments to protect themselves from other nations. Boundaries and borders are everywhere.

In this particular place there is a spirit of fear which seems to affect all. Many of the older generation are afraid to walk the city streets at night and little children are continually being warned not to speak to strangers. I find such things sad.

Even more strange, in a world of almost infinite variety, many of these human creatures seem to fear those who are different. They appear suspicious of those who are of a different colour. I should explain, beloved Pzylon, that the humans on this planet have different skin tinctures with colours of black, white, pink, red, brown, yellow and many shades in between. You and I know that the Creator loves colour as the works of his hand shows, but these human creatures cannot live happily together as varied creatures of the same Creator. It is all so very strange.

But, even more bewildering, many of these human creatures do not believe in a Creator. Is not that beyond all understanding? With their own eyes they see the wonders of their world all around, with their minds they can comprehend the works of creation, but they do not believe in a Creator! Indeed they themselves mirror the Creator's power in a small way by being able to build and devise and manufacture but even the wisest of them seem to believe only in a sort of 'once upon a time' story. With no blush of shame for such foolishness, they say, 'Once upon a time there was a Big Bang and all things, good and bad, weak and strong, came to be.'

In our homeland we would not insult the intelligence or imagination of our children by telling them such idle tales. But here it seems to be intellectually acceptable to believe that an infinitely complex universe came about through mindless forces. They seem to accept that their very understanding has come about through chance! It is as if they pride themselves so much in their own greatness and superiority on this planet that they consider that there can nowhere be any being greater than themselves. No Creator! Can I be blamed for being bewildered?

A great sickness seems to have overtaken mankind and infected all creation. Even the best of these human creatures have been affected because the good are capable of being bad. Indeed, they have a tendency to corrupt the purest things for their perverted pleasure and to twist innocent joys into a means of satisfying their own lusts. How can I understand such things? It is beyond all my experience.

So I do not like this place. It is dark and perplexing and I am continually in danger of drifting into despair.

However, be assured, beloved Pzylon, that my sense of duty will make me stay here until my work is done. I am beginning to know how hard and painful that will be. Already I am longing to return and be at home in those realms of peace and glory where I belong.

Reading over this report I can only apologize for the way in which my emotional reactions have confused my observations. I may well find that things are not really as bad as they appear. I know not. Certainly I cannot escape the fact that there is beauty and glory here. In days to come I may find much to lift my heart and come to know that good has not departed from the face of the Earth. But it is too early for any glib conclusions.

As I get to know these human creatures, and become more familiar with this place, my reports should be more lucid. Doubtless you will be hoping so! Meanwhile, as I suggested at the start of this first report, my mind is so troubled with the things I have seen and heard that it is difficult for me to think clearly and organize my thoughts and impressions. I trust that you will understand my problem, beloved and patient Pzylon.

But be assured I do not like this place. That, I must confess, is my initial conclusion. Here good seems to be tainted by evil, glory is tarnished by pain, and even beauty is blemished. I do not know if I love, loathe or pity these human creatures. It is all so very sad, strange and bewildering.

Give my love to those I have left behind in my sweet homeland. May peace and harmony be with you all.

Beauty and Blasphemy

Greetings. Sadly I must confess that my mind is no more tranquil than when I compiled my first report. There is so much here to destroy my peace of mind. This is not only a place of good and evil, it is also a place of beauty and blasphemy. Two experiences recently have shown me that this is true.

I walked through the poorer part of the town, which is what they call these living areas where they dwell together in communities. Against the sky, surrounded by deserted wastelands, great machinery and buildings lie empty and abandoned. Where previously, it seems these human creatures drilled and mined into the earth to extract its richness, where they had communally toiled to construct and manufacture, now all stood derelict and silent. Whether this is due to technological change, political decrees or economic forces, I know not.

Dwelling places, which they call houses, still stood around these areas of dereliction, some boarded up as if awaiting demolition but others were still occupied. Little children played happily on the litter strewn streets but the whole scene was ugly. Obscene graffiti defaced the walls; senseless slogans and unknown initials. It was as if someone was anxious to leave his mark in an uncaring universe by asserting, 'I have

13

been here.' It seemed a place of dirt and despair.

I could only walk with a growing depression in my heart. It was as if the vandals had triumphed, destroying all traces of beauty or glory. Then I saw a stagnant pool surrounded by a broken enclosure. Around were the rusting remains of two and four-wheeled vehicles, prams for babies and bursting cardboard boxes spilling out some of the rubbish of this throwaway, materialistic culture. It seemed to be some sort of unofficial dumping ground. (Dump! That is what they call these places. Is not even the sound of it depressing?) That little hollow seemed a denial of the beauties of the garden of creation. Even the water in the little pool appeared to be so polluted that nothing could possibly live in it. It was a declaration of ugliness.

But beside that stagnant pool, amongst the decaying rubbish, was a lovely sight. Vibrant, and bravely declaring its unlikely existence, was a flowering rose bush. Blood red roses lifted their shining beauty to the sun. It reminded me with a flash of joy that the Creator of all beautiful things will not, cannot be defeated. He sprinkles the grass with daisies and buttercups and makes roses flourish where death and decay seem triumphant. That rose bush lifted my spirits from the depths of despair. Beauty has not departed from the garden of his creation.

The Creator is good to all his subjects, even to such an unworthy servant as myself, or to these rebellious human creatures. They are indeed rebellious, as my next experience showed.

Having seen those roses in all their loveliness, I retraced my steps into the town. Passing through the shopping centre, a busy, turbulent place where market transactions occur and where many young earthlings gather, I became caught up with a large crowd of young men. They were excited, shouting loudly and walking briskly together in a large, jostling group.

It became obvious they were going to a sporting event, known as a football match, not to take part in such a health-giving exercise but as spectators. They were festooned in the bright colours which distinguished the team which they supported, with gaudily-decorated scarves, jerseys and rosettes pinned to their chests like medals. It is difficult to explain why, but they brought with them an air of menace. Fear rose in my breast.

It was not hard to imagine this mob rampaging through the streets, destroying everything with a fierce and happy abandonment. I felt that, with this group, only the law of the wild places would prevail. But I may have misjudged them. Whether they were aware of it or not, each of those young men carried the image of the Creator within him. Individually they may have been kind, decent human beings, but as a mob I found them frightening.

They shouted, chanted and sang, making a raucous noise rather than music. But the songs they sang were not in praise of life, youth, love or even the Creator. They sang in adulation of their team which, time after time, they vowed to support into eternity - for evermore! It was as if they wanted to spend their afterlife watching, supporting and praising their team. I found it all difficult to understand.

The shouting and singing may have been harmless, for the young must have some way of dispatching their excess energy. It was the language used that deeply troubled me. Between snatches of songs they shouted to one another, and to those passing, and they used words in ways I had never heard before.

They used the foulest of language, exchanging obscenities and blasphemies with fearsome intensity. This brutal, vulgar language, a syntax of evil, was horror to my ears. The obscene words disturbed me but the casual use of blasphemy pained my heart.

Although many earthlings do not believe in the existence of the Creator, he is not forgotten. These human creatures have an instinct to call on him in times of peril. I would expect this from such image-bearers, but I did not expect to hear the Creator's glorious name used in evil abandonment. It was used by those young football supporters as an idle curse, a thoughtless oath, almost as a defiant cry of rebellion. Why did they use the name of the good Creator in such fashion? I cannot tell.

There have been many evil men on this planet - men who have murdered, plundered and raped without mercy. The history of this place is littered with the names of the cruel and heartless.

Alexander the Great and Attila the Hun ruthlessly conquered by force of arms. Genghis Khan ravished a continent. Napoleon killed hundreds of thousands for his own greater glory. Nearer the present age on this planet there have been men like Stalin, Hitler and Mussolini who were agents of death and eliminated millions of innocent men, women and even little children. All human history is stained with blood shed by such evil men.

However, their names are not used when human creatures want to express hatred or anger. Instead, they use the good and great Creator's name, or the name of the only true good man who walked this Earth - the

Young Prince of Glory who is known here as Jesus Christ. It is those divine names which are used as thoughtless curses or idle oaths. It is all so very strange. How can I understand such things?

I could only separate myself from these young football supporters as quickly as possible. I did not belong to their number. Indeed, I am very much aware that I do not belong to this place. At times I am troubled by the thought that I will never be able to understand these human creatures or really fully comprehend what is actually going on in this strange place. It is all so very difficult for me.

I confess, beloved Pzylon, I am so near to despair. But fear not, I will do my duty. That rose bush, blossoming in beauty among the rubbish in this ruined garden of creation, did indeed cheer my heart. But so many of the words, and so much of the works of these human creatures, can only depress and sadden my heart.

How I long to be with you in that bright homeland of ours where, but no, I will not write of it - such words would only further darken my heart and cloud my spirit.

But I do trust that peace and harmony will continue to be with you.

Darkness and Bewilderment

Shamar to Pzylon: Earth Report 3

Greetings, and thank you, beloved Pzylon, for your concern and advice. I know I should do as you suggest and try to concentrate on one aspect of human life in each report and also to seek the good as well as the bad. This, I accept, is good advice. However, my spirit must be calmer before I can be a truly objective observer. Sadly, my spirit is far from calm. Perhaps I am still dazzled by the glory I have left or blinded by the darkness I see here. I know not. You must forgive my failings as I struggle to come to terms with my experiences of this place.

Everything on Earth seems to be contradictory. These human creatures, although they know they must die, live as if they will remain on Earth for ever. Many spend all their strength and life acquiring material things and collecting riches for themselves. My initial impression is that they have a very materialistic culture.

There can be no doubt that they have a genuine love of beauty but they litter their streets with the debris of throw-away rubbish. They have built grey and characterless housing estates for themselves which they now recognise as 'concrete jungles'.

In their hearts they know that they should love one another but all around I find suspicion, distrust and hate. I find it all beyond my understanding.

Last night I walked through a town and it was an experience of pain too great for words. As you advised, dear Pzylon, I allowed my sensitivities to reveal the events of the night in many hearts. Perhaps it was a mistake but the impressions flooded my mind and there was no escape. The unseen glance, the unheard whisper, the silent prayer, the stifled curse, all converged upon my mind so clearly that this being of mine ached with the pain they expressed.

A young couple pursued a quarrel long into the night - thoughtless words of hate and bitterness driving out the love they once had known. Their child sobbed loudly from a nightmare and the shrill words coming from the other room but no one comforted him.

A drunk man lay cursing in his sleep while his wife, old before her time, wept silently at his side.

In a corner house, drawn curtains hid a family from the outside world but nothing could hide their weary lovelessness from my penetrating senses. An old woman lay dying, her mind wandering in the sun-drenched fields of her childhood. The son lay on a sofa, eyes fixed on a paperback book which had a picture of a nude woman on its cover. By the dying embers of a fire his wife sat knitting, her eyes screwed up in concentration as she followed the complicated pattern on her lap. The old woman on the bed opened her eyes suddenly and painfully moved her parched lips as she croaked for a drink of water. 'Water - drink,' she breathed hoarsely and, unheeded, died thirsty.

It was as if every house carried its own secret sorrow. A young girl wept for the unborn child growing within her and feared the reaction of her parents and even the boyish father of the child. A sleepless man lay on his bed dreading the arrival of the auditors on the morrow. He would be sure to be found out and there was no hope. An old woman lay with dry eyes but burning tears dripped painfully from her heart. Tomorrow the ambulance would come and her future lay in a geriatric ward of the local hospital. A young man sat on the edge of his lonely bed and toyed with the bottle of pills in his hand. It would be so easy. Just a drowsiness and then a sleep of peace. They would all be sorry then!

A young couple spoke of a party that had just ended. Bottles were arrayed on the sideboard and table. Glasses and cigarette ends littered the fireplace. In a corner the record player still buzzed. 'A great night. A great night,' declared the young man, emptying the glass in his hands. Sprawled on the sofa was the young woman, glassy eyed, and lipstick smeared across her cheeks. She splashed some wine into a tumbler and drank greedily. 'I'm drunk,' she muttered and then laughed almost hysterically. 'No more nights like this when your wife gets out of hospital, eh?' Again she laughed as if she found it all funny. The man took another gulp from another glass. 'A great night. A great night,' he answered.

Pzylon, beloved Pzylon, it was such a frightening experience! I saw, I felt, I knew it all. I can only record but a fraction of the fragments of nightmares, cries of pain and fear mingling with hopeless longings and half-formed dreams that assailed me on that dark and lonely walk. I could only walk away from the town with tears burning their way down my cheeks. But I did not know if I was weeping for these pitiful human creatures or in self-pity for finding myself in such a dark and depressing place.

I do not like it here. It is a strange and terrible place.

Earthlings are so foolish. Their lives were surely meant to be exciting adventures, joyous journeys of discovery, and not wearisome endurance tests. If these people are not sick then they must indeed be foolish beyond my understanding.

Perhaps this experience, though painful, has been good for me. It has taught me not to open myself completely to these human creatures but to remember my task here is simply to observe and report. I will try to do as you so wisely suggested and concentrate on specific aspects of human life and living. And I know this must include the good as well as the bad.

I know the Creator must have his own people even in this ruined paradise. Jesus Christ, who we know as the Young Prince of Glory, must still be calling men and women, young and old, to follow and serve him, so there must be some who have responded to his call. Doubtless I will find them and be able to report on their activities in due course.

But sadly, at least from my first impressions, the followers of the Prince do not appear to have much influence on this society's moral or cultural climate. However, I know it is too early in my task for any final judgment to be made. However, it almost seems as if this place is under the control of the Evil One. But such a thing cannot be, can it?

The Creator must be sovereign, ruling over all. He cannot be a mere spectator watching the works of his hand. Undoubtedly these human creatures have been given free will and allowed to rebel. I have seen the result and it is painful to behold. If they will not love their Maker how can they love one another?

Enough for now, dear Pzylon. I am tired. Peace and harmony be with you.

Families and Fragments

Greetings from a lonely servant. You have no idea how loneliness weighs on my heart in this place. But, to my surprise, I find I am not alone in experiencing the pains of alienation here. Although this planet is teeming with life, there are many human creatures suffering the agony of isolation. It is sad to see.

The Creator has made these human creatures gregarious so that they can only find fulfilment in being with one another. Indeed, he has set them in families. So, although they live as members of a tribe or nation, it is only the family which gives identity and character to the individual. I want to report on the family - a rich source of blessing for these human creatures.

The family begins in marriage. There is a ceremony in which a mature male and female earthling vow publicly to love and remain faithful to each other until separated by the curse of death. From that moment onwards they belong to one another. The two become one because their lives become so entwined that the union makes a unity. Marriage is a glorious institution which shows the wisdom and compassion of the Creator. It provides love, companionship, physical and social satisfaction, and much else for these lonely human creatures. It is within this bond of marriage that sexual desires can find their true consummation.

It is also within this covenant of love that children are born. In a family circle an earthling child can learn, in the most natural way, individuality and responsibilities to others. It is through daily experience that the child discovers how to relate to others while developing as an individual and unique creature. There seems to be a consensus of opinion that good family life provides enrichment for all earthlings.

That is the ideal. On this planet the reality is different. Here I am pained by the sight of so many families fragmenting, marriage vows being discarded and the ancient, yet still relevant, laws of the Creator ignored. It is all very sad.

However, there are good families here. They are a joy to behold! I have seen families out walking - little girls holding their father's hands possessively, little boys sharing their discoveries of life with interested parents. I have observed fathers romping on the grass with their children, rediscovering the joys of their own childhood. I have watched tired women patiently telling bedtime stories to their little ones. And I have seen husbands and wives whose love is so strong that even death itself will not break it. The love of a man for a woman, and a woman for a man, has not departed from this place.

Sadly, however, I must report that all is not well in the realms of family love and faithfulness. Something like one in three earthling marriages are broken by divorce. The laws of this place make it easy for couples to decide they no longer want to live within the marriage bond so their vows are treated as if they had never been made.

Dear Pzylon, this society seems to be suffering from the malaise of moral anarchy. There certainly appears to be a great confusion in the realm of sexual behaviour: 'adulterer' and 'adulteress' are now apparently archaic words in earthling language. Even that which is against human nature, men with men and women with women, is considered socially acceptable. I find it all sad and strange.

Many earthling books, magazines, and probably most of the cultural trend setters here, seem united in suggesting there is nothing wrong with sexual intercourse outside the marriage contract. They only warn of the dangers of sexually-transmitted disease. Earthlings seem to believe that they can do as they like providing it does not mean physical illness. How can that be a good principle for a good society?

In addition, a growing number of human couples live together without the public exchange and commitment of marriage vows. I find this bewildering. Surely even on this planet true love delights in being betrothed and pledged to another? There cannot be real love without commitment. Licence and love cannot be comfortable bedfellows.

I am continually finding it strange how these human creatures completely ignore the teachings of the Creator and his Son, the Young Prince of Glory. How painful it must have been for him to have lived amongst them. Whilst on this planet he warned them against lusting after one another and therefore committing adultery in their hearts. When I see the sort of magazines and books on open display here I can only wonder how much mental adultery is being deliberately created by this culture. It is not simply that awe and mystery have been taken away from sex.

24

Romance and beauty also seem to have departed. This cannot be for good.

In spite of the widespread encouragement and use of birth-control methods and abortion many human babies are born out of wedlock. This means that many children are not born into a natural earthling family. Also the growing number of divorces deprives children of a united family. All this means there is an increasing number of what are called 'One-parent families'. I confess that this phrase seems a contradiction in terms to me but it is widely used here.

I am fully aware, beloved Pzylon, that it is early yet in my attempt to understand these human creatures but I think there is much here which is not working for the good of a healthy family life.

Discipline is not popular amongst human creatures. I have seen little earthling children being allowed to choose their own books and magazines without parental guidance. Many are left to decide which television programmes they will watch. I have observed boys and girls, scarcely above the age of puberty, being allowed to have evening, or all night parties without parental supervision or interest. It is as if these parents have resigned their moral responsibilities and handed their children over to the guidance of professional entertainers, advertising agents or the manipulation of the media. (I must report on these forces later.)

As I have hinted before, human creatures live in a very materialistic society. They seem to see the chief purpose of man as the acquisition of possessions and then enjoying them for as long as they remain in fashion. Young human couples, on setting up their first home, are encouraged to burden themselves with debt so that they can have many things. It is not what you and I would call a recipe for peace of mind.

So, from the earliest, earthling children are encouraged to be acquisitive. A materialistic society quickly teaches them to equate 'I want' with 'I need'. I find it all confusing.

Earthling family life is a sharing life, but materialism is a selfish philosophy. Surely, if human children are not brought up to share with the family they know, how can they ever learn to share with the human family they do not know?

But, as you and I know, Pzylon, sharing goes much deeper than mere possessions. Many families here do not even share time together. Parents and children often have so many outside interests that they are rarely together as a family. Individuals in the family go their own way and do their own thing. It seems to me that few families play together, walk together, visit together, or even spend time with one another. Such earthling families are fragmented. Even if they do play games together they are usually being competitive rather than co-operative. Winning becomes more important than having fun! Is this for the good of earthling family life? I suspect not, but I may be wrong.

Perhaps there is hope. Many human creatures are becoming aware that all is not well with the earthling family. But if they persist in ignoring the rules of the Creator the confusion will certainly continue.

Sadly, many here dismiss the idea of a Creator and his rules and claim to be able to solve every problem themselves. This is a planet with a proliferation of experts! So, for problems in human family life there are marriage guidance experts, child behavioural experts, sexologists, sociologists, psychologists and psychiatrists. Countless books are published offering advice on every aspect of private and family life. Doubtless they have some primitive wisdom to impart but often I have observed that they simply compound the problems. I cannot believe the Creator intended earthling family life to be so complicated that it requires more than love and common sense to survive and prosper.

Beloved and patient Pzylon, I apologise if this report is confusing you. I am not finding it easy to understand what is really happening in this place and to these human creatures. I only know I do not belong here. Of course, I may have been observing the wrong families or misreading the evidence. But, as I have looked and considered the family scene, it does seem to me that even the best earthling families are under pressure. It is certainly a time of great cultural change and moral confusion for them.

In this situation it is not surprising that so many human families are struggling to survive. Rather than being surprised at the fragmentation of earthling family life, perhaps I should be pleasantly surprised at the number of their families which I observe surviving and thriving. It may be another sign that good has not departed from this strange place.

When I consider what kind of life these human creatures could enjoy - and then compare it with what they actually do - it brings me close to despair. However, I will faithfully continue my observations and reports.

As always, I wish you what is sadly lacking in this strange place - peace and harmony.

Idleness and Boredom

Shamar to Pzylon: Earth Report 5

Greetings from a strange and bewildering planet. I appreciate your sincere concern and words of encouragement which will help me to acquire a calm mind. It is not easy. However, I am slowly learning to control my emotions and sensitivities as I survey this place and people. I know I must accept these human creatures and judge them by their own standards, but while I may accept, I doubt if I will ever approve. I am still unsure whether these human creatures are positively evil or just stupid! Perhaps both conditions are much the same. Certainly it is not clever to be evil.

I still find much here to confuse me. This report will illustrate what I mean.

There is much work to be done on this planet. The garden of creation needs continual care and human creatures are obviously intended to serve and help one another. But, by some peculiar reasoning, the human creatures in this place seem to equate work with financial reward. Only if they are paid for their labour are they said to be 'working'.

This sort of thinking leads to some ridiculous conclusions. It means, in this country anyway, that a woman who cares faithfully for her husband and children is not considered to be a 'worker'! She may labour hard from morning until late at night, keeping the house clean and warm, shopping, cooking, baking, washing, ironing and engaged in many other domestic duties, but these are not seen as 'work'. Is not that strange to our understanding of communal life?

However, here there are many men and women who are not in paid employment. Many are young people who have never known steady employment. They are the unemployed and many seem unable to cope with time on their hands. I will illustrate what I mean and this should please you, dear Pzylon. You asked me to include more specific details in my reports rather than vague analysis!

Arthur is nineteen years of age and is unemployed. He has not been in any form of paid employment for almost two years and spends most of his time alone in his own room.

Each day he wastes the long hours lying on top of his bed listening to the local radio station on his transistorised receiver. This provides almost endless music which is only briefly punctuated by the forced jollity of presenters who are known as 'disc-jockeys'.

These 'disc-jockeys' have achieved spurious popularity by their apparent ability to say nothing of any importance in a most entertaining way. They are professionally jovial and merry, a sort of electronic jesters.

Arthur is in an almost perpetual state of boredom. Increasingly, he is becoming remote from his family and friends. Sad to say, his family shows little interest in him. His father works in a local steelworks and devotes most of his spare time to the game of bowls - outdoors in summer, indoors in winter. Arthur's mother works as a cleaner of some offices and spends almost every evening at the bingo and social club. These are places where it appears that older humans congregate.

They talk, they drink alcohol and they spend money merely in an attempt to win money in return - a strange entertainment. The only other member of the family, a daughter, seems to spend her time at discos and cultivating boyfriends. These discos are places where people meet to dance to music. At such places it is very important to look attractive as it is impossible to make friends through conversation - nobody can speak above the noise of the music. This often suits the young people as many are shy of talking to others. It is strange that great noise is cultivated so that silence can be maintained.

To get back to my subject: Arthur is alone and lonely. He spends most of his time indoors and takes no physical exercise. He is thin with a pale complexion and, rather than showing the bloom and vigour of youth, he has the listlessness of old age.

I have great sympathy for Arthur but find it hard to understand his behaviour. He has withdrawn into himself and seems to have lost interest in everything and everybody. It is most strange because there is so much that he could do.

In a wooden hut behind the house Arthur has what human creatures call a bicycle. It would take him less than fifteen minutes to cycle out of town and into the countryside where he could find refreshment in the beauties of creation.

In a cupboard beneath his bedroom lies a forgotten fishing rod which humans use with great intricacy to catch fish and he lives within walking distance of a river teeming with fish. In the same cupboard, now gathering dust, lies a stringed instrument called a guitar on which he once started to learn to make music.

Beneath his bed, in various cupboards, and scattered around his room are the unused remains of the many hobbies he started to become interested in during his short life. These include stamp collecting, model building, photography, jigsaws, books and innumerable games and pastime activities.

At the end of the street where Arthur lives there is a building holding nothing but books called a public library where he could plunder the wisdom of the ages and freely borrow books on a wide variety of earthling subjects. There is a sports centre in his town where, because he is not in paid employment, Arthur could have free entry. There are many youth clubs with healthy and interesting activities organised by the local governing body.

A large number of repair and painting jobs are required to be done in his home. The garden needs attention with the lawn overgrown and the weeds thick in the flowerbeds.

But I have observed that Arthur does not go cycling, fishing, or return to any of his old hobbies. He never reads a book, takes part in any sporting activities or busies himself with any repairs around the house or garden.

Day after day and night after night he merely lies prone on his bed and lets the incessant beat of cheap music drive all thought from his mind. He does not even indulge in daydreaming nor let his imagination wander through the landscapes of his mind and out into the infinities of creation. The golden hours of youth are being washed away on a tide of music which neither inspires his heart, stimulates his imagination nor strengthens his will.

The life of Arthur, like all human creatures, holds

such promise. But it has become a nothing. His life has become largely meaningless. I find it sad.

Surely the Creator does not want his earthling creatures to experience a life such as Arthur is living? Something is wrong somewhere. I know it is too easy to condemn but hard to understand. Perhaps that is my problem. I can see what is happening to Arthur and others like him, but I do not fully understand why it should be. How can I?

Certainly I do not understand the Earth's economic system which means that many, young and old, cannot find paid employment. How can I appreciate any system where the meaning of work is to be found in wages? Then, certainly, I cannot know what makes Arthur act the way he does.

But the picture of him, lying in his little room, thoughtlessly listening to his music, haunts me. I know it is not right and should not be. He is not living as a truly human creature, rejoicing in his gifts, senses and imagination.

But which earthling has failed Arthur? Parents? Politicians? Economists? Educators? Moralists? Society? Or has Arthur brought all his miseries on himself? I know not. Perhaps they are all to blame. Perhaps the fault lies deep in the souls of these human creatures with their twisted values and peculiarly destructive way of life. All I know is that I want to weep bitter tears for these sad creatures. I want to tell them to stand up, open their eyes and live.

However, I am not here to blame or find fault. I can only observe and report. All I know is that seeing Arthur and others like him has touched my heart and troubled my mind. He is missing so much. The gift of life was given to be enjoyed, not endured. It was meant to be excitingly accepted and not to be suffered as a thoughtless, emotionally deprived existence. The good Creator surely wants all creatures to rejoice in all the gifts in his good creation.

Perhaps, dear Pzylon, I should add that there are other young people, and some not so young, who are unemployed but are living inventive and fulfilling lives. In many hearts the human spirit seems capable of triumphing over all forms of adversity.

But I will not forget Arthur who has a disembodied radio voice and recorded music as his only companions. With all creation to explore, all his life to live, he lies on a crumpled bed doing nothing. It is all a tragic waste. I find it infinitely sad.

I can but wish you that for which I long - peace and harmony.

Television and Trivia

Shamar to Pzylon: Earth Report 6

Greetings from this place where, it seems to me, confusion reigns. Again I thank you for the kind words of encouragement you have sent me. However, I must confess that new impressions and sensations are still bombarding my mind and emotions, and my feelings and thoughts are still in a state of flux. It will take some time for me to become used to this cultural and social climate - though may the good Creator forbid that I should ever become part of it! But I will strive to do my duty.

After my initial shock at being amongst these human creatures on this strange planet, I have been spending some time alone. Of course, I have not been neglecting my duties. What I have been doing is spending hour after hour watching television. Therefore, this report is about television and trivia.

Watching television appears to be the main recreational activity here. In the early morning, throughout the day, and far into the night, these human creatures sit engrossed in front of their television sets, and the viewing figures are startling. (This is a great place for statistics and surveys but they are often both informative and confusing!) These show that 98% of the homes in this society have television sets and these are switched on for an average of forty hours a week. As I have mentioned, many homes have the habit of having the flickering pictures on continually in the corner of the living room, whether or not they are watching. Actual viewing figures suggest these human creatures watch television from three to five hours each day. These figures are for earthling adults. Children appear to watch more. Television is indeed lord of many lives and homes.

Whilst I find these figures surprising I am even more astonished to find that many consider television to be a neutral medium. Some, wise in the ways of the world, insist that watching television has no influence on the thought patterns or behaviour of these human creatures. Such arguments are beyond my understanding. Here there are rational and spiritual creatures who, day after day, week after week, through all the long years of their lives, watch this medium and it has absolutely no effect on them! How could such a thing be?

Certainly television is a powerful medium for communication. It can bring pictures of all the world into the living room and show life in all its diversity. But it is a one-way communication. The viewer must sit passive and receive what is being provided. Apart from any emotional or mental reaction, the viewer cannot respond in any active way. In a sense the viewer is simply a receiver.

I believe it must be very difficult for these human creatures to be rationally critical when watching any programme. A continuous stream of audio-visual impressions assaults their eyes and ears and allows no time for rational reflection. It is slick, easy on the eye, appeals to the emotions and holds attention by pace and change. So the viewers need do nothing but let the electronic pictures transport them away from a weary world.

As I understand it, the stated aim of earthling television is to supply information, education and entertainment. In spite of these noble aims I have found the medium mainly devoted to entertainment and escapism.

There is a bewildering variety of programmes continually on offer. It is a kaleidoscope of brutal realism and escapist fantasy. At times I found it difficult to distinguish between the two but my thought processes differ from these human creatures so they do not suffer from the same confusion. I am not certain, but for earthlings, fantasy sometimes seems more real than reality.

A mass medium must appeal to the masses. Programmes are designed to appeal to the great mass of earthlings of widely differing educational and cultural backgrounds. This creates pressure to make everything attractive. Fact and fiction, drama and entertainment, religion and news, must all be presented so that they grip the audience and hold their attention. I suspect boredom is the prime sin on earthling television. Everything must be an interesting show.

This means it is assumed to be necessary to give human creatures what they want. If viewers are happiest with silly panel games, scantily-dressed girls, bright music and sexual innuendo, then that is what should be provided. Immediate thrills and sensations must be supplied. Culture, in the sense of the best of the past and present, is treated here as a minority interest.

I found myself wondering about this attitude. If an earthling forgets his past, loses his memory, then he is without identity. When a nation forgets or ignores its past, is it not in danger of losing its identity? Then, as all earthlings know, a prolonged diet of cheap food only creates an appetite for nothing but cheap food. I suspect this is also true of mental stimulation. Only the good creates a desire for more good.

In all this, beloved Pzylon, you must be thinking that I am condemning television as worthless and evil. I confess I do not like it but I hesitate to condemn it outright. There are two reasons for this hesitation.

The first reason is that, as a creature of the Creator, I cannot condemn relaxation and recreation. This is the way all his creatures are made - able to relax and escape the cares of daily life with its many burdens. Perhaps on a sin-wrecked Earth, leisure and escapism are even more necessary for these poor human creatures. Entertainment and recreation may be good for them but, I must wonder, can endless escapism be for the good of any creature?

The second reason why I cannot condemn earthling television in itself is that it must be a gift from the Creator. The possibility of transmitting sounds and pictures throughout this planet was placed in creation and these human creatures simply discovered it. He must have placed it there for them to find. Surely the good Creator made nothing evil in his creation? He must have given this medium of communication for the enriching and enobling of human life. He cannot have meant it to be an evasion rather than an exploration of what it means to be human. Television cannot be evil in itself.

But, as I have sadly discovered on this strange planet, these human creatures can take good gifts and use them for that which is not good. This, I rather suspect, is what has happened with the medium of television.

Of course, there are informative and educational programmes on television. I have seen some of them and they helped me to understand some things about this place and culture. Some helped to reveal the common humanity of these creatures and did illuminate something of the diversity and glory of this planet. But most programmes did tend to concentrate on the trivial and I cannot see how they can be a good and healthy influence on the culture and daily living of these human creatures.

As with so much in this place, I found it depressing and troublesome. By concentrating so much on television I felt vaguely deprived. I was aware that there was a whole world to explore, people to get to know, places to go, things to see and all I was doing was sitting idly watching pictures on a little box in the corner of a room. I sensed in some ways I was wasting my time here and, as we know, time itself is a good gift from the Creator's hand.

Perhaps some of these human creatures feel the same way as I do about their evening watching television. I know not.

There is much more I could report about this dominating medium of communication but I am tired. Tired, not only of television, but of this planet and people.

I still long for the day when I can return to my bright and fair homeland where the shadows of this planet are unknown. Until that day comes I will, as promised, do my duty.

As always, may peace and harmony be with you.

Entertainment and Escapism

Shamar to Pzylon: Earth Report 7

Greetings, and I stand rebuked. You are right in your criticism and I have no words of defence. It was an astonishing lapse on my part - I told you all about television except the actual programmes that are presented. This hurried report is an attempt to remedy that omission.

Last evening, like millions of others in this place, I spent hours watching earthling television. I did not find it a particularly inspiring experience but there were moments when I felt I was adding to my knowledge of these humans. Sadly those moments were few. Mostly it was entertainment and escapism. But enough of generalisations and let me simply record what I saw and my reactions to it.

The first programme was *The News* - or at least they make it plural presumably to emphasize how much of it there is. News seems to be such a dominant and important feature of this culture that I would like to report on it more fully at a later date. All I will say here is that earthlings were treated to a portrayal of events from all around their world. Whether this leads to a greater awareness of the brotherhood of man and a common humanity, or is only a form of dramatic entertainment, I am not sure. But more of that in a later report.

After the news there was a short film about a subject they call 'nature-study'. It proved to be an engrossing record of breath-taking beauty and showed something of the rich variety of life-forms which inhabit this planet. Creatures of the sea and land were shown in their natural surroundings. It was like a celebration of creation. Indeed, it could have been a moving tribute to the Creator of all things but, and this pained my heart, that was not the intention of the film makers.

I was almost lost in admiration for the makers of this film. For mere earthlings, their patience, imaginative ability and artistry were beyond compare. But it was a programme about the living creation and the Creator was not even mentioned. We were called on to admire the ability of the beautiful creatures to adapt and evolve to suit the environment in which they found themselves.

It was hard to follow this type of thinking and it may be that I do not yet understand the thought patterns of these human creatures. But the implications behind the commentary were clear. Animals, fish, and presumably birds, have adapted their biological structures to survive. They keep changing so that the species may continue. In simple words - the creatures become their own creators! How can such things be?

Another confusing thing about this wonderful film was the frequent use of the word 'nature'. It was never actually defined so I am unsure of the intended meaning. It seemed to be used to define the creation but, at other times, as if it was the Creator. At one point the narrator used the phrase 'Mother Nature' as if she was some sort of feminine deity. But these human creatures do not seem to believe in a god. It was all very confusing.

However, the film about the animals and fish was excellent and enriching to my mind. It was only later I realised that it would have been even more enjoyable if I had turned down the sound and simply watched the pictures. It was the commentary that disturbed my peace of mind.

· The film was immediately followed by a programme for young earthlings. Apart from a few introductory remarks it was almost entirely devoted to their own particular brand of music and depicted the type of place which Arthur's sister whom I mentioned in a previous report frequented.

It was loud with an insistent beat that seemed to lack harmony and variation. Many groups and singers presented musical pieces but, at least to my ears, the basic tune never seemed to change. Perhaps I am not attuned to the melodies and music of this place and this makes it difficult for me to give a valid critique. I found this programme most strange. Its name derives from its popularity - *pop* - and this is certainly true with the young human creatures of this place. Perhaps I should try to report on it more fully sometime. ·

Certain things struck me whilst watching this programme of popular music. As I have said, the tune never seemed to change and the vocal quality and accents of the singers also seemed similiar. Also I found the dress of the performers most strange. Some were outrageously dressed, others simply dowdy and gaudy. Most were dressed in old or cast off clothes and some had their faces painted and their hair coloured in vivid hues. It was most strange to my eyes. The audience seemed no better dressed. Perhaps it all had some tribal significance which I do not understand.

To the incessant beat of the music there was dancing. At least I can only presume it was dancing. It seemed to me that what these young creatures call dancing is not a measured, aesthetically pleasing and sensuous movement of the body but rather a frenzied agitation which appears to be an explosion of primitive emotions. The music seemed to excite them into savage, almost violent movements as if in an uncontrollable passion. I found the scenes disturbing as they lacked what you and I, dear Pzylon, would consider art and grace. But perhaps I am still a poor judge of this culture.

Occasionally, the cameras concentrated on individual faces amongst the audience and dancers. Being the faces of the young I expected them to be bright, expectant and tinged with wonder. It was not so. Most of the faces, performers, dancers and audience alike, were devoid of expression and seemed to reveal a pained emptiness. It was as if there was no life behind the facial features of their humanity. I found it depressing.

As you and I know, (and many memories of our homeland still burn in my mind), communal singing, music making and dancing can be uplifting and inspiring. Such things can lift weary hearts and thrill the mind. This music programme for the young earthlings did not seem to be doing that for them, or for me.

The next programme I saw on television was trumpeted as the *Film of the Week*. It was a war film which reinforced my suspicion that these human creatures really treat life very cheaply. As a war film, full of fury and savagery, it showed pain and death in many guises. The violence portrayed was sickening in its detailed realism of humanly inflicted suffering.

The plot was about two brothers, both army commanders, who were fighting on different fronts on the same battlefield. Each was determined to capture a certain town before the other. So they took many unnecessary risks and made their men suffer and die to achieve their evil ambitions. The brothers were driven by envy and jealousy of each other rather than by the struggle for truth and justice.

Perhaps it could be argued that the film showed the folly of jealousy and the evils of war but these concepts did not come across to me. The plot was obviously an excuse for the action and the action took over the message. It seemed to me that the carnage of war was presented as a form of brutal entertainment. I did not like it. Can earthlings really consider it entertaining to sit and watch limbs being severed, bodies being blown to pieces and violence in all its forms assaulting helpless creatures? No, I did not like it, but such films seem to be enjoyable to many of these human creatures.

The film was followed by another news bulletin which seemed largely a repeat of the earlier reports of disasters and crimes. How these human creatures must love bad news! Surely this cannot be a planet where there is nothing but evil to report?

After the news (and the equally depressing weather forecast!) there was a play. Of course, I am not familiar with the dramatic conventions of this culture but my impression of this play was that it was evilly trivial.

It was the story of a young married woman who had begun to suspect that her husband was being unfaithful to her. So, in revenge, she deliberately seduced a much younger man and began an affair with him. Many of the scenes took place in the bedroom with the characters in various stages of undress. Little was left to the imagination. As viewers we were invited to become voyeurs. The dialogue was punctuated by casual blasphemy and what seemed to me to be little more than the basest language. The denouement was the young wife discovering that her husband was not having an affair with another woman - it was another man who was his lover!

The play was basically a dramatisation, almost a celebration, of moral nihilism. The concepts of right and wrong were neither examined nor explored. Indeed, the underlying assumption was that all things were permissible and the only true value was individual happiness. Frustration and unhappiness are the only sins and grace is to be found in self-gratification.

Perhaps I misunderstood the message of the play but, to my understanding, it seemed neither good nor true. It did not seem to widen or deepen my understanding of the human condition in any positive sense but only convinced me of its negativity. Perhaps that is what they are trying to express. What I do find confusing is how these human creatures seem to find entertainment in nudity, adultery and violence portrayed and dramatised. Can that be healthy? I did not find earthling television inspiring or uplifting. I did not like it!

And I have not mentioned the adverts. Between the programmes and often interrupting them, came the loud, sonorous voices of men, or the soft, seductive tones of women, commanding or imploring earthlings to buy things. With the voices were short imaginative films to encourage them to buy. There was always the implication that they deserved such luxuries or that their lives would be infinitely impoverished if they could not have them.

These adverts had their own fascination. It must be like finding one's home turned into a market place where each stall-holder tries to shout louder than the other. The aim was obviously to convince the unthinking viewer that the goods and services offered were really of priceless value and that life without them could not be worth living.

The uses and techniques of advertising are among the subjects I must seriously consider in my observations. They reveal much about the values of earthling society. I must compile a fuller report on advertising at a later date.

Beloved Pzylon, as you will appreciate from this report, it was with relief that I turned off the television set. It was largely an evening of escapism and entertainment. At least, it seemed to be what these human creatures see as entertainment. There is the possibility that I had a particularly bad evening for my viewing experiment but I doubt it. It all seemed so trivial.

I am aware that I have reported more on my own reactions rather than on a detailed content of the programmes. I make no apology for this for my reactions are surely part of my observations.

Perhaps this popular medium of communication is really for our experts to study. It would be a simple matter for me to gather programme material and forward it for a more learned study by those wiser than I ever hope to be. You can let me know if this is desirable.

Meanwhile, dear Pzylon, I still long to be with you again. May peace and harmony be with you.

Poor Little Bad Boy

Shamar to Pzylon: Earth Report 8

Greetings from this bewildering place. I think I reported something of the confusing moral standards on television. Well, that confusion is certainly reflected in earthling society. Whether their mass media is responsible for, or simply reflecting and perhaps reinforcing, the current moral standards I know not. But I must report on a particularly harrowing incident which I witnessed and followed to its distressful conclusion. Like me, you will find it almost unbelievable.

Mrs Sutton is an earthling widow of over seventy years of age. She was 'mugged' earlier this month. In this place 'mugging' is a colloquialism for robbery with violence on the streets. Usually it is a crime against the old and frail. It is a sad story.

Rarely did Mrs Sutton go out at night, particularly on her own. Indeed, in the cities and towns of this place few of the human elderly go out alone in the dark. There seems to be a fear of it. But one evening Mrs Sutton heard that a friend had suddenly lost her husband through the curse of death. She felt that she had to go and offer sympathy and comfort.

After visiting her friend, and sharing some tears with her, Mrs Sutton left to go home. She walked as quickly as her aged legs would allow and tried to ignore the knot of fear in her breast. It was with a sense of relief she turned into her own street. It was then that it happened.

A young earthling man sprang out of the darkness. He hit her full in the face with a clenched fist as the other hand grabbed her handbag. As blood spurted from her nose she fell over a small hedge. The young man ran off carrying her handbag which only contained a few pounds.

It was providential, but the young man ran straight into the arms of two approaching law-guardians. He was caught. Mrs Sutton was taken to the local hospital where, after treatment, she was detained overnight for medical observation. Apart from a bruised eye and bleeding nose her injuries consisted mainly of nervous shock.

All this was bad enough but it is the sequel to that incident which has deeply troubled me. Police inquiries have shown that the young man has a very unhappy, almost unnatural background. He was only a few months old when his father left never to return. Over the years his mother has lived with a number of men, none of whom took any interest in him. He has a number of brothers and sisters, probably all from different fathers. It is the sad story of a fragmented earthling family being a burden, not only to itself, but to the community.

So the young man was guilty of assault and was known to the police for previous acts of petty theft and vandalism. There can be no doubt he is a most unfortunate human creature who is not only cursed with the sickness of evil but is greatly in need of help.

Rightly or wrongly, I know not, the court of law which sat in judgment on his behaviour decided to treat him as a 'poor little bad boy'. So he has been placed on 'probation' which means he will be under the supervision of a servant of the court for the next year. The resources of earthling society are being brought into play to help him live a more socially acceptable life.

Now, since the crime of mugging poor Mrs Sutton, I have observed that the young man has had two visits from his 'probation officer'; a 'social worker' has been to try to help his family's life, and an 'employment officer' is attempting to secure suitable paid employment for him. I can only hope these agents of society can succeed in their efforts. The sad young man is, like all human creatures, capable of being a worthy citizen.

I have serious questions in my mind as to whether the fact of guilt and human responsibility have been made clear to this young earthling. But that is not what has troubled me most.

What seems to me to be the strangest part of the whole incident is simply this - nothing has been done to help Mrs Sutton. This strange place seems to have the social machinery to deal with the attacker but not the attacked. I find this bewildering. Apart from the policeman who took Mrs Sutton to hospital, and later returned to take an official statement, no one in authority has been to see her. Is not that strange?

Certainly Mrs Sutton has been to see her medical doctor twice. Although sympathetic, he is a very busy man and could only give her a few minutes of his time. He prescribed some tranquilizers and sleeping pills. But now Mrs Sutton lives in an almost continual state of nervous tension. She is in terror of the dark and, at times, is even afraid to go out during the day. In spite of the sleeping pills she finds it difficult to have a full night's rest. She is very much on her own and apparently there is no one to help. No 'social worker' or 'health medical advisor' has come to offer assistance or advice. Even worse, she is neglected by her own family.

Her only daughter is married and lives some fifty miles away. She came to visit her mother the day after she was discharged from hospital but, in spite of promises, has not returned. Occasionally she phones and has sent flowers to her mother but although the flowers may be beautiful they do not provide companionship to a frightened old woman and bring little comfort to her fears. Mrs Sutton's son, who lives nearby, has called in to see her twice, each time in rather a rush and unable to stay. He is a very busy man. As I previously reported, families in this place are strangely fragmented. I find it infinitely sad.

The people who live around Mrs Sutton's house do not see themselves as their neighbour's keeper. Indeed, her only visitor who had the time to sit and talk was her recently widowed friend.

What can I say about all this? What can I say about a society which has caring agencies to help the law-breaker but apparently has nothing to help the victim? What can I say about humans who do not act humanely, or sons and daughters who care little for their mother? Is it any wonder that words fail me? It is all so bewildering to my mind and heart. Need I report once more that I do not like this place?

The Good Creator did not mean life to be like this. Of that I am sure. Even from these muddled words of my reports you must know, beloved Pzylon, how I long for the peace and harmony in which life was meant to be lived.

News Action and Reaction

Shamar to Pzylon: Earth Report 9

Greetings and, believe me, I value your words of wisdom and will try to take your advice to live as you suggest. But it will not be easy.

I know that I should not become emotionally involved here in this sad place but how can I remain a mere observer when I see what is going on? The things I have seen and heard, the experience that shattered Mrs. Sutton, have affected me deeply. How can it be otherwise? The Creator has made me a creature with sensitivity and sympathy - would it not be a denial of my creaturehood if I deliberately suppressed these faculties?

But enough of my problems, I have my report to make. Earlier I promised some observations on how 'news' is treated in this place. If I report on this aspect of television it will show you something of my dilemma.

These human creatures appear to have an obsession for news. They seem to want to know immediately what is happening everywhere. It is like a drug to which they are addicted. Newspapers are taken in to almost every earthling home, radio gives hourly broadcasts of news summaries with occasional longer bulletins, and television provides a regular diet of news.

Television is more immediate, more exciting, than any other medium portraying the news. In the morning, early afternoon, evening and night, television has a full news survey with many updates during the day. This service must show how important news is to these human creatures.

There are usually two talkers reading the news on television and, I must say, they are normally presentable people. The women news readers are young, tending to glamour rather than maturity, and the men handsome in a masculine sort of way. No earthling whose face is deeply lined with the experience of old age ever seems to read the news on television. This is interesting and must be deliberate policy. Perhaps it is part of the showmanship which governs much of television. I know not.

The immediate introduction to television news bulletins, and the first sight of the news readers, is heralded by urgent music or the solemn chiming of bells. This makes it sound as if the fate of the nation is about to be announced.

What is then reported is, I suspect, only a repeat, with minor variations, of all the news since the curse of disobedience invaded this planet. It is really little more than a catalogue of deaths and disasters and all sorts of outrages against the innocent. In glorious colour, earthlings can see the effects of bombs exploding and bullets flying. Brutal actions make the best pictures.

Then they are shown leaders around the world angrily proclaiming their desire for peace! Governors of the people promise better times but, in spite of the professional sincerity in their voices, I doubt if any earthlings believe their words.

Interspersed with these solemn and sometimes horrendous events were pictures of the family of royalty going on holiday. (I may add that this has no connection with the Prince of Glory but is rather some historical institution by which one family is revered.) Then a 'film star,' who is not a celestial being but a mere human who is employed to pretend to be someone else, was getting married for the sixth time. The funeral of a policeman who had been killed by terrorists was shown next. Then, to conclude the diet of news, there was a delightful cameo of the wedding of two severely handicapped people. They were holding hands as they came out of the church in their wheelchairs. It was a kaleidoscope of unrelated events.

I found it all mentally confusing and was unable to cope with the emotional response demanded by the medium. The action of the news presented to me caused a bewildering reaction on my part. I wanted to weep at the violence and death I saw portrayed on that little screen. When I saw the film star - whoever she was - getting married for the sixth time, my emotions were turbulent. Indeed, I was not sure what emotional reaction should be mine. Should I rejoice that these human creatures still want to be united as man and wife? Should I weep because she has had five other husbands whom she vowed to love until death? Or should I be troubled by the mob surrounding the wedding party. Those fans undoubtedly idolised, almost worshipped her. But in my emotional confusion there was no time to analyse my reactions because almost immediately the presenters moved on to another story.

Anger, tears, horror and pity were my immediate reactions to scenes at the funeral of the murdered earthling policeman. The cameras showed his young widow being helped into the church and, in graphic detail we saw her pretty face distorted with tears and grief. My response was again bewilderment. Had the whole nation the right to witness those tears?

Surely grief is a private and personal matter and not something to be placarded to the world? Earlier in the same news programme I had heard a reporter questioning a policy maker who asserted that, 'The public have a right to know'. This may be true but I wonder if there is a corresponding right not to know. Should all have a right to know, and see in living colour, another's tears, sorrow and mourning? I contrasted it, I am afraid, with our sensitivities which we always use to sympathise with what is inside, what is unseen. Earthlings seem to wish all feelings to be displayed and broadcast at all times. Such things on earthling television troubled me.

Then I was not sure how to react emotionally when I saw a pack of news reporters interviewing a poor mother whose daughter had been sexually assaulted and murdered. She was asked, 'How did you feel when you heard that your daughter had been raped before she was murdered?' Anger and bewilderment swept over me at these words. I do not think I could have ever imagined them being put to any poor woman in such a situation, but I heard them with my own ears. Such things are completely beyond my understanding. Can you blame me for not liking it here?

These news bulletins arouse in me such a welter of emotions that they threaten to engulf me. Within less than half an hour I felt pity and sorrow, anger and horror, sympathy and despair, love and pleasure. It was too much. The range of emotions stimulated by those news pictures overwhelmed me. How can these human creatures cope with it? Indeed, how can any created creature cope with such assaults on their senses and emotions?

Pzylon, I hesitate to make this suggestion, but it does seem to me that the only way to cope with such a bombardment of bad news is to become desensitized. Surely these human creatures were not made to deal with such emotional pressures and, if not, then for their own mental and emotional ability they must become numb? In this way they can look on the news as a show which need not concern them greatly as individuals. But I am not sure how this can be. It is all too much for me.

In watching the televised news I found one other obvious fact - it is predominantly bad. It appears that 'bad' is news whilst 'good' is scarcely worth reporting. I must confess I find this scale of values hard to understand.

Some of those wise in the ways of Earth have suggested that the mass media has made the whole world into a global village. The theory seems to be based on the fact that primitive man sat around the village fire and exchanged news and transmitted culture in a casual and informal way. Now the media envelopes the Earth the whole world has become a global village.

This may be true but there is one point that troubles me about this theory. When, around the village fire, earthlings exchanged news, they must have reported the good as well as the bad. Surely they talked of the many happy things that happened and not simply of the evils that are the lot of mankind? Would they not have recounted stories of unselfish deeds and joyful events? I would have thought this would be so.

As you will see, beloved Pzylon, I find it all so hard to understand. Perhaps these human creatures are beyond me. I am not sure whether their television, and particularly its treatment of news, has helped me to a fuller understanding of this strange planet and its equally strange inhabitants.

After trying to assimilate the television news and general run of programmes, I have another disturbing thought. Are these human creatures being turned into spectators of life rather than participants? Television makes them viewers with no control over events and I am not sure if this can be for their good in making them as they were designed to be.

Finally, I found the most crucial question of all kept haunting my mind as I watched the televised news. Was it true? Did it really happen as I saw it on the screen? I could not help wondering if it was all really factual and true. You and I know that seeing is not believing and even on this planet a straight rod placed in a tub of water will appear to be bent. The eyes can deceive the mind.

Then I know, though it may be denied here, that earthling television is not a window on the world. It is a photographic recorder taking a picture and, behind that photographic recorder is a director saying what is to be photographed. It is a deliberate selection of reality and even that is edited before it is screened. Interviews and film reports are obviously cut down to fit the timescale allowed so some things are left out. In this way the truth can be easily distorted. Perhaps such thoughts are cynical, or an unfair distrust of earthlings employed in television, but this question of truth keeps intruding into my mind. Questions like: 'Was the whole city in uproar? Was I only seeing one small street?' or 'Am I seeing the whole event or only dramatised versions of it?' There was no way I could confirm that what I was seeing was true or real. However, as I keep trying to remind myself, I am only an observer here. Perhaps these human creatures can cope much better than I can ever hope to do. Certainly their news, and particularly their television news, is very popular here and is watched by millions of them.

But, as this report must make clear, I did not find the televised news to be either inspiring or encouraging. Rather it depressed me. It made me feel that this world seems largely without hope. But this cannot be. However, I do not like this place.

The depression that has continually hovered over my mind since coming here is once more threatening to engulf me. I can only retreat into my memories and meditate on the glories I have known and will know again.

Now I must end this report promising that I will be faithful to my duties as an observer. Meanwhile remember me before the throne of him who is the only source of all joy and beauty.

May the harmonious hope of my homeland soon be also found in this place.

The Bad and the Good

Greetings from your servant who once again stands rebuked. Your strong words of reprimand, although hurtful to my heart, were probably timely. There can be little doubt that this place is affecting my judgement although I know not how this can be avoided. I can only promise to wrestle with this tendency and try to be more objective in my observations.

Perhaps you are right, beloved Pzylon. I do seem to have fallen into the very pattern which so disturbed me on the human television medium - reporting only the bad news. But, even in admitting this truth, I do think I should answer your charge of my becoming obsessed with the wrong I see.

In defence I can only say that the experience of being here is intensely depressing. Previously I had only known continuous joy in an enchanted realm and to come into this place is a traumatic ordeal. To encounter the wrong when previously I had only known the right is painful beyond belief. I am appalled by some of the things I have heard and seen in this sad place. It is not what I expected or could ever have imagined. Earth really is a troubled planet.

However, as you so forcefully reminded me, I had earlier reported this place to be one of glory and horror and suggested that human life is a bewildering mixture of good and evil, pleasure and pain. So I confess that, since that previous report, I have tended to concentrate on the bad rather than the good. In this I am not sure whether to apologise or defend my position. Perhaps it is the evil that demands my attention whilst I take good for granted. Indeed, this may explain their media with its emphasis on the bad. I know not.

All I can say is that I do not like this place. I am sure that my reports are reflecting this fact.

My problem is that these human creatures have a great capacity for good. They love, and can make and do beautiful things. But all seems to be tinged with corruption. There appears to be something wrong at the heart of everyone and everything and this, as you will appreciate, is utterly beyond my comprehension.

However, I can understand why you, beloved Pzylon, should ask me to report on the good and the joy I have found here. I recognise this is essential for any understanding of this planet and is probably necessary for my own peace of mind. Whatever impression I may have given in the past, or I may give in the future, be assured that there are elements of glory and good to be found here. Indeed, I have seen them with my own eyes.

In spite of the cruel practise of murdering some babies even before they are born, many are warmly welcomed into the world. I have seen earthling babies, even some unsightly with physical handicaps, being welcomed with love and joy. I have observed a mother, her eyes moist with love, cradling a newborn baby in her arms as she whispered in the maternal language that needs no words. I have watched a father, his plain face transformed with love and wonder, lift his newborn child with gentle hands. Such scenes show a tender joy.

It is most strange but these human creatures, at such moments, find tears are never far away. Intense joy and happiness seem to bring a hint of tears to human eyes. Why this should be I do not know, but it is a fact. Perhaps it is a sort of sorrow for the paradise that was meant to be. It may be that, if only instinctively, they are aware that human life should always be one of joy and happiness and they can only weep for its sad reality. They are bringing this bundle of potential, of hopefulness into a hopeless world. All I can say is that these humans are strange creatures. Certainly I cannot say I understand them.

They have a remarkable capacity for self-sacrifice. Earthling mothers willingly deny themselves for the good of their children and fathers will do without for the sake of their family. This certainly is true of many of them. Some will even selflessly risk their lives for the sake of others.

Recently, near this place, a little girl fell into a fast-flowing river. The friends with whom she had been playing screamed in helpless terror and a man walking nearby heard their cries. On seeing the plight of the little girl in the river he immediately tore off his jacket and dived into the water. He was able to save the life of the little child.

Rather to my surprise, when the little girl's father and mother arrived and were occupied in comforting their daughter, the man hurried away. He did not even wait for a word of thanks. Is not something like that good news from this sad planet? That man acted with no thought for his own safety and without any desire for reward.

It seems that these human creatures instinctively care for one another and will risk much to maintain or save the life of another. They must recognize somehow that their lives are their most precious possession even though what they do and what they believe appear to deny the fact. Doubtless this must be the way the Good Creator has made them, and they belong to one another whether they acknowledge it or not.

I have another item to report which illustrates this reality and - you will be pleased to learn, Pzylon, it also is good news. Earlier I reported on the experience of an old woman, Mrs Sutton, who had been cruelly treated by a young criminal and then rather callously treated by the community. There has been an interesting development in her story.

There is a local youth club, which is where some young folk go in the evenings (although many seem to prefer standing outside to going in!) in Mrs Sutton's neighbourhood. They heard about her frightening experience and decided to try to help. So a group of these young humans, little more than boys and girls, visited Mrs Sutton. They gave her a bouquet of flowers and a box of groceries. The young men then offered to tidy her overgrown garden and the girls expressed a willingness to help with shopping or housework. Mrs Sutton, after recovering from her initial suspicion, was quite overwhelmed by their kindness. This new experience has made her realise afresh that good has not departed from her world. This I know is something you want me to keep in mind in these reports.

These young humans have now become friends of Mrs Sutton and, by their actions have shown that all young humans are not alike. But the thoughtful actions of these young people have gone completely unnoticed, and unreported in the media. It is not cynicism that makes me suspect that if they had laid seige to her home and created havoc it would have earned wide publicity.

However, the caring action of these young human creatures has cheered my heart. I think that they, perhaps without being aware of the fact, were actually suffering from communal guilt and this dictated their actions. One of their generation had offended the laws of the community and the commandments of the Creator, so perhaps they felt the sting of guilt and tried to make amends. In time I may learn to understand better the actions of these human creatures.

At the moment I am not sure that this sense of communal reponsibility and guilt is a common awareness. The general ethos here seems more designed for the preservation of rights rather than responsibilities. There is much talk of human rights but little of human responsibility. I certainly find this confusing. Something is seriously wrong in human life with its current values and standards, but, as I have now reported, some good keeps breaking through.

Seeing the actions of that youth club has reminded me of something you have mentioned more than once, beloved Pzylon. I have not spent any time with the People of the Prince. I can assure you I know that they are here, but first I want to observe and comment on the culture and society which shape the accepted standards of this place. Although I am finding so much that is contradictory perhaps the fault does not lie with me. It may be that this society is out of joint.

I will, in due time, report on those who serve the Creator but I suspect that the glory will still be stained. After all, the Prince when he lived on this planet went about doing good. But he found it an evil place. Indeed

I have discovered a terrible, horrible thing - these humans dared to capture and execute the Young Prince of Glory! But I must write of this at another time.

So please, Pzylon, allow me to make my reports in my own way. Perhaps I am not as organized as you would like but I am trying to be faithful and, if the bad outweighs the good in my observations, then that is how I see it. But I will try to be faithful to my duty and as objective as possible.

Advertising and Promises

As ever, warm greetings from your lonely observer. If I remember correctly I promised to report on the extent and influence of advertising in this place. At least, I think I did! As you know, record-keeping has never been my strong point!

The medium of advertising is very influential here. It is a simple but interesting earthling activity which is easily defined. When the makers or suppliers of goods and services want to inform others what they have to offer, they use advertising. I certainly can find no fault with the principle and worth of this enterprise. It is good that human creatures can be informed about what is best suited to their needs. So the purpose of advertising is good.

Unfortunately, as in so many areas here, there is a gap between the principle and the practice. This report will show what I mean, as it is obvious, at least to me, that human advertising is designed to have an emotional rather than a rational impact and is often unrelated to the item displayed.

The most immediate feature of their advertising that struck me was its extent. Adverts are everywhere. There are large, attractive pictures at street corners and various places where earthlings congregate. Advertisers must be clever as they have used the earthling habit of *waiting* to their advantage. The humans *wait* for fuel for their vehicles: they *wait* to be transported by what are known as buses and railways: they *wait* in queues of other vehicles in order to proceed. Many buses and other transporters - taxis and lorries - seem to be little more than mobile displays with their advertising signs and slogans. (Maybe that is why so many of the goods shown are other vehicles - merely bigger and better than the human creature owns himself.) Many shops use bright cards with fluorescent colours and flashing lights to publicise their goods. Anything up to half the content of newspapers is given over to adverts. Indeed, some local newspapers consist of nothing else. The postal and telephone services which humans use for communication are also used with the aim of persuading them to buy and keep on buying. As I have mentioned, on some of the television channels there are audio-visual adverts. Commercial radio also has brief breaks when shrill and excited voices shout to convince earthlings to buy their goods.

Since coming to this strange place I have found it impossible to escape the sights and sounds of advertising. The voice of the *adman* is heard throughout the land.

It seems as if the most gifted human artists, musicians, and writers are now employed as *admen*. Music, art, poetry, drama and all the other earthling arts appear to be reduced to the encouragement of consumerism. I suspect that the most imaginative of human minds are at the disposal of the advertising industry.

With simple words they can weave phrases and slogans that quickly become the common coinage of human language. They can make startling images that penetrate the heart and lodge in the mind and be for-ever associated with some product or other. They can compose musical jingles that lodge deep in the human memory so that adults and children can unconsciously sing the praises of some alcoholic beverage or manufac-tured artefact. Then they can, with skill and dramatic ability, use the medium to tell a story, create memorable characters, and transmit an influential message - all in less than a minute of time. It is as if the most skilled art is in the service of money.

All the emotions of these human creatures are used and exploited for the purpose of salesmanship. They are made to appeal to their sexual and maternal instincts, or to awaken their unhealthy desires of envy, greed or fear. It is all a strange fantasy which I find beyond my understanding but, I must confess, I have found it all fascinating. The adverts on earthling television are simple but profound.

I saw a woman, a mother with an unlined face, not a hair out of place, staring in sorrow at muddy clothes. How can she restore them to cleanliness and purity? A voice from above tells her to use a certain type of detergent and miraculously it appears. She uses it to wash the clothes and they come out shining white. It is a nice little story with a happy ending to encourage other human women, if they care for their families, to follow her example. Perhaps it is the twist of my mind but I found it a sort of parody, rather than a parable, of the cleansing which can only come from above.

I watched a young woman, shyly conscious of facial spots or unruly hair, being transformed into a glamorous beauty with the use of particular skin creams, shampoos or hairsprays. With the application of such cosmetics the girl finds that every male eye lights up on seeing her. Again it is a cosy, romantic story. It suggested to me, and doubtless to some earthlings that renewal and re-creation are allegedly found in the application of cosmetic technology.

It is the same when men are portrayed in these adverts. Bashful young men discover that a new perfumed cosmetic or health product will make their dream world come true and glamorous young women will throw themselves into their arms with almost sexual abandonment. Or they can find true masculinity by gulping down alcoholic beverages. As I observed previously, immense importance is placed upon the external appearance of one earthling to another. Judgments concerning personality or marital suitability are formed it seems, on the first glance!

In other advertisements tiny babies gurgle with delight when they are dusted with certain talcum powders or allowed the right nappies. Little children eat with hungry enjoyment the latest processed, convenience foods that are advertised. Domestic bliss is found in having the latest kitchen stocked with the latest appliances and the home furnished with the latest styles. And so it goes on and on.

It is all a fantasy which offers an impossible life in a dream world. It is a promise of health, beauty, status, sexual attractiveness, social acceptance and true masculinity or femininity. It is an offer of salvation, the promise of a new creation where human beings can be new creatures and find all secret wishes coming true. Perhaps when so much of their world is harsh and hopeless, the earthling turns to these ideas. He absorbs them faithfully like an innocent child, endeavouring to forget that the reality of his situation is very different. The alarming thing is that of course he cannot forget, but remains dissatisfied and angry that his world is so different from his dreams. Indeed, it is not products that are offered, but these distant dreams.

I know that the Creator has given these human creatures the ability to dream and this must be a rich gift. But what happens when they are encouraged to dream the wrong dreams? Should earthlings be inspired to dream that true life is to be found in acquiring the things that are advertised at great expense? Is feminine attractiveness really only a matter of fashions, scents, cosmetics and style? Is genuine masculinity really to be found in expensive cosmetics or in hearty drinking where there is no thirst. Can the love of a human mother only be shown by the detergent she uses to wash her children's clothes? Does a happy earthling childhood consist solely in having the right toys to play with and the right confectioneries to eat? Is married bliss for these humans merely a matter of furnishings and foods? To judge by many of the adverts this is so.

Please do not misunderstand me, my dear Pzylon. I know that food, drink and clothes are important to these humans. But we know, and the Young Prince of Glory told these humans long ago, that life is more than clothes, food and drink. But so much of the advertising industry seems to be implying that the Prince was wrong and that true life is to be found in the abundance of possessions. I find it sad.

It may seem strange to you but these human creatures appear to enjoy the adverts. I certainly find it bewildering that any creature should find enjoyment in being manipulated. But many of the adverts are interesting, intriguing and imaginative. They are often witty and have striking images and memorable slogans and sometimes appear little more than an extension of the entertainment scene. But, in the earthling world of commerce, where money is the measure of all things, advertisements are made to sell.

So they are cleverly cunning in their approach. The adverts may be amusing or dramatic but they carry their own message. Images, words and music, are used to innocently penetrate the heart and mind. There they lodge and remain long in the earthling's memory. The desire is cunningly planted - a desire for things!

There can be no doubt that advertisements do produce desires and wants. Indeed, I find it significant that there are no advertising campaigns for the necessities of life. Always it seems to be for the frills and fancies of human existence so that luxuries are presented as necessities. This means, I suspect, that in many human minds there is a confusion between needs and wants so that they are made to believe that if they want something they must need it. I find it all rather sad.

I could go on but, as in all things here, the subject troubles me. It grieves my heart to see men and women with obviously great artistic gifts using their talents to sell soaps, powders, pills and drink. It depresses me to see artists and craftsmen dedicating their abilities to persuade others to buy the trivialities and technological toys of this culture.

Again I find myself in a dichotomy of thought. As I have said at the begining of this report, I cannot believe that advertising is wrong. But I do not like the way in which it is conducted here. Perhaps it would be an interesting exercise if I tried to work out the place, purpose and techniques that advertising should be engaged in for the real good of these human creatures. I would like to see them treated as rational, responsible beings rather than consumers to be brainwashed. But I am too tired to attempt such thinking. I really am tired of this planet, place and people.

Pzylon, is it possible that I am the wrong choice for this assignment? Please consider this as a possibility and advise me accordingly. Meanwhile I will continue to do my duty as best I can.

With heavy heart, and longing for the day when I can return to the glories of my homeland, I send you my fervent wish that you may continue to know peace and harmony.

Everything and Nothing

Shamar to Pzylon: Earth Report 12

Greetings from a humbled heart. I accept your strong
words of criticism although they pained me with the
sting of truth.

My thoughtless questioning of my calling here is
sincerely regretted. I know that I must faithfully do my
duty irrespective of my personal emotions. I am also
aware that feelings are irrelevant to duties. Forgive me,
beloved Pzylon, if in my occasional despondency I give
expression to unworthy emotions. For a sensitive soul,
such as the Creator has made me, my duties here are a
burden. Knowing the best it is depressing to be confronted with the worst.

The pain I have found in observing the activities of the
'admen' comes from seeing some of the effects of their
work. I have seen earthling families and individuals
deluded into believing the promises of the adverts and
have found no real satisfaction. Having been encouraged to want everything they have discovered that often
having everything means nothing. Many of these
human creatures have not yet learned that life is much
more than material possessions - though these are important and necessary to creatures of the Earth. I am not
against these things - how could I be when the Creator
has given so many things to enjoy? But the 'admen'
are continually composing psalms in praise of the

accumulation of things and assuring earthlings that materialism is the only path to enjoyable living. Many human creatures are caught in this sad illusion.

Let me report on the Callington family. They may not be typical of all families but they do illustrate a real problem.

Edgar Callington and his wife, Lena, live in a large country house on the outskirts of a picturesque little village. They have two children - Peter who is twenty years of age and at university which is where some human youths go to study; but what actually occurs there seems to be shrouded in some mystery; and Pamela who is two years younger and is spending a year at home whilst considering her future.

They are, on the surface, a very successful family and have everything that is generally considered necessary to make life sweet and good. In a word, they are affluent. They have a large house, three cars, at least two holidays a year abroad, and apparently none of the family ever wants for anything.

Although both Edgar and Lena came from rather poor beginnings they certainly have progressed in the world. Edgar boasts of being a 'self-made' man. Driven by a ceaseless ambition to get on, he feels that he has arrived, in that he is now managing director of a large company which owes much of its success to him. But this means that he spends much of his time travelling around the country and occasionally abroad. He thinks of little but his work and even when home spends most of his time in his study with his papers or on the telephone. He has little contact with his family.

The mother, Lena, loves having an active social life and is proud of being a good hostess when entertaining her husband's clients or business associates. This does not entail a great deal of work as she has a daily help in the house and private caterers when giving a party. She is proud of her home which she has furnished according to the latest designs in the glossy magazines she loves to read. She carefully cultivates her leisure time and is a member of the local golf club.

Although Peter, the son, is at university working for a degree in business studies, he really has no idea of what he wants to do or be. It was his father who insisted he take up business studies as a means of 'getting on in the world'. But Peter has little contact with his father. Indeed, a fellow student once told an anecdote about what happened when he was out fishing with his father and Peter confessed, 'Do you know, I have never been out alone with my father in my life!'

Pamela, the daughter, is having a year off studies so that she can decide whether to go on to university or college and what to study there. But in truth she is doing no thinking. She is just enjoying being free of commitments and is currently obsessed with horses and some stable lads who work nearby.

They appear to be a family who have everything. But they are not really happy. Indeed, I fear for their future. A diet of materialism cannot lead to healthy humans or satisfy the human heart. So, although the future is hidden from my eyes, I fear for the Callington family.

The father is now a worried man. A large international industrial company is trying to take over his firm and, if this succeeds, he has no idea what it will mean for him. He has always lived beyond his income and worked every possible hour he could. He finds himself being assailed by two contradictory emotions for he is becoming tired of the endless hassle and grind of his workload and yet he dreads having nothing to do. He is an un-happy man.

Lena, his wife, is aware that she now has everything she ever dreamt of having but now, to her surprise, is increasingly dissatisfied with her lot in life. She still feels young and yet has the nagging sense of life passing her by. In a word, she is bored. A new golf professional has come to the club and gives her the impression he would like to be more than just an acquaintance. Now she is daring to dream of breaking her marriage vows to her husband and committing adultery with him - it would add spice and adventure to her life.

At university, the Callington's son, Peter, is finding himself listening to lectures and reading books whilst wondering what it all has to do with real life. He has the sense of going through the motions of life rather than living. He has found a source of cheap drugs and has experimented with trying to find some sort of transcend-ental experience that will bring some savour to the business of living.

Pamela, the daughter, is a worried girl. She suspects that she is pregnant and has really no idea what to do. Never having been close to her mother, Pamela has never seriously considered taking her fears and worries to her mother and talking it out. She can imagine her mother saying, 'Why on earth didn't you take the pill?' which is the means humans have of chemically ensur-ing that unwanted offspring do not result from their sexual union. Then her mother would quickly arrange an abortion.

As I have reported, I do not know the future of the Callington family. The shape of their future is in their own hands under the sovereign will of the great Crea-tor who rules on high. But the problems the future must bring or solve are not caused by their riches but by their attitudes, the lifestyle they have embraced and the way they concentrate on their own selfish desires and wishes. Regarding the children, Peter and Pamela, my heart weeps for them. It must be the law of the Creator's universe because it is a fact of life here - the children suffer for what the parents do wrong.

Of course, all earthling families are not as the Callingtons but many are tainted with the same disease which has gripped them. It is a sort of self-centred materialism encouraged by the pressures of this culture and fed by the promises of the 'admen'.

Young couples marry, taking on large debts on a house and furnishing their home beyond their means. They can enjoy things now and worry about paying for them later. Shops give out cards which represent money. With these, earthlings appear to be willing to pay more than the cost of goods, merely for the convenience. These cards the shops seem to supply on demand. Banks, which once existed to encourage earthlings to save, now use all sorts of advertising to encourage human creatures to go into debt. I find it all so very sad.

What a strange and bewildering place this Earth is! At times I simply do not know what to make of it all. But this I do know - the good Creator never intended his creatures to live beneath burdens of worries and fears. Why have they rebelled against him? This, at root, must be the cause of all their problems and perplexities. I know he has not deserted this place. He sent his Son, the Young Prince of Glory, to this planet to be the Son of Man and lead these human creatures to full and glorious life.

I must tell you I saw an Earth sunset last night. It was

a truly awesome sight. The sun was a glowing orb of gold sinking beneath the horizon and the whole sky seemed to be melting into a myriad of colours. It was a sight of dazzling splendour. Truly he is the Creator of beauty and glory. How can these creatures see such things and not humble their hearts and worship the Maker of such ravishing loveliness? It is all so strange and beyond my understanding. But, although I cannot understand this sad place, I can catch glimpses of eternal peace. This sunset was such a moment.

May you continue to know that true peace and harmony which the Creator delights to give.

Newspapers and Gossip

Shamar to Pzylon: Earth Report 13

As always - greetings. But again I must begin with an apology! Looking back over the subjects I have covered in my reports I am disturbed to find I have not considered newspapers. This is probably another example of my lack of organisation and, if I may add, the confusion this place is having on my mind.

I have already reported on how these human creatures have a strange obsession with news. They seem to have an insatiable desire to know all the details of all that is happening in their world.

Television is not the only popular medium catering for this desire. Newspapers are also in this business. I have found earthling newspapers interesting as they illuminate my attempts to understand these creatures and their culture.

It seems to me that newspapers have a great advantage over the electronic medium of television. Readers are not bombarded with quickly changing, audio-visual images but have time to consider and assimilate the various reports that are presented. Also, of course, they can be read and re-read. But this is something for the more academic to consider.

But what are they? you ask. They are large volumed books full of varied information (and some advertisements) which are produced every day on thin, low quality paper. All earthlings seem to try and read them.

I have been surprised at the wide choice of newspapers available here for they seem designed to cover a broad range of understanding ability. But the newspapers which are read daily can be divided into two types - quality and popular. These adjectives describe their content and circulation.

The quality earthling newspapers try to provide a service for the thinking reader by giving a more detailed analysis of events. They certainly have far more reading columns than the popular newspapers. This means that they have greater depth to the stories they cover and report on a wider area of national and international events. They also give space for background articles on current affairs and the issues of the day. I do not believe that they are perfect. By definition, the reporting of news should be a neutral activity but it rarely is. The reporter or editor usually has some sort of political belief into which most stories fit. However, I must say that the quality earthling newspapers do seem to try to provide a service of information to help a rational being make some sense of the affairs of this planet.

The truly amazing thing is how so many newspapers can tell the same stories in so many different ways. I suppose I should be intrigued by their 'imaginative' reporting rather than merely shocked by their twists and fabrications.

Compared with the popular newspapers, the quality papers do not have large circulations. However, they have influence because they are generally read by those humans in authority and the intellectual trend setters. But, for the general culture of this place, the popular newspapers must have the greatest influence. They must help to shape and direct the thoughts of millions.

The popular papers are sold in vast numbers. Almost every earthling home seems to get a morning paper, many buy evening papers and, on Sunday mornings, some homes purchase several newspapers. Acres of forests are being taken from this Earth to supply this demand for daily newspapers. Certainly it is a demand, for reading newspapers almost amounts to a national pastime here!

Although these popular papers - known as tabloids because of their size - are called newspapers I have doubts as to whether they are in the business of news. They seem to be more part of the entertainment industry. They provide an interesting or exciting way to begin the day.

The front pages are not columns of news but are often covered with pictures or huge black lettering proclaiming the main point of a story alongside. (These 'headlines' as they are called appear to promise more than they deliver.) There are also specially selected details about all the good things to be found on the inside pages which will titillate and thrill. Then, often, there are particulars of simple numbers games where readers can win fantastic sums of money.

Where they report on the great issues of the day these are usually personalized or even trivialized so that no earthling need be troubled by the complexities of the problems on this planet. It seems to me that reality is presented in as entertaining or exciting a way as possible.

The inside pages are liberally sprinkled with pictures, cartoons, and many portray a semi-nude woman in photographic detail. Why this is done I am not quite sure but it apparently pleases the male readers who must get some sort of pleasurable satisfaction from looking at the mammary glands of an unknown female earthling. This is obviously associated with an infantile craving for the mother's breast or perhaps it is something to do with these human creatures and sexual desires, I know not. I leave this fact for analysis by those more expert in this field.

This blatant emphasis on nudity, or semi-nudity, troubles me. It seems to be degrading to these female creatures, reducing them to mere sexual objects to provide sexual fantasies for the males. It must encourage the dangers of mental adultery or, at least, some dissatisfaction in some men's minds. I wonder if they look at these pictures and then at their wives and feel cheated by their lot in life. But it may be that I do not fully understand these human creatures. Certainly I find everything so strange.

In general, these tabloids go in for what is called 'human interest' stories - that is, stories about people. While this would seem commendable, in effect it seems to mean stories of scandal and shame. Nothing seems to bring forth greater headlines than reports of the famous humans some of which I have referred to previously - pop music stars, television performers, sportsmen or film stars - being involved in adulterous associations, drugs which artificially induce the extreme heightening or dampening of a human's mental state, or some such activity. Readers seem to love being informed of the scandals of the rich and famous. I am not sure if such things add to the sum total of earthling knowledge or illumine what it means to be human.

In fact, I see these tabloids as gossip sheets rather than conveyers of real news. The activities of the human creatures are fascinating, even for themselves. But I am not sure that concentrating on the dark side of their actions is worthy of being placarded in banner headlines for daily reading. It is not as if this is done as a warning to others: it appears, rather, to be a form of celebration. It is all beyond my understanding.

I must make one further comment on the treatment of sex and scandal in which so many of these tabloids specialize. Often the papers which portray glamorous girls in varying degrees of undress also take a very hard line regarding sex crimes. At times, next to detailed photos of half-naked girls, I have found fierce calls for ruthless vengeance on those who assaulted the female of the species, in which they call them 'beasts' and 'animals'. I find this bewildering for animals do not really behave like humans. Even more confusing to my mind is the fact that many scientists, holding to the theory of evolution, have been preaching for over a century that human beings are only animals anyway.

So I find the tabloids to be presenting a strange code of moral contradiction in that they are the purveyors of immorality preaching the needs of morality. They unashamedly show pictures of naked women and then express horror that some human creatures violate the bodies of females. It is all so very bewildering to an observer such as I am.

I fear that you will again accuse me of concentrating on the dark side of life among these human creatures on this strange planet. I cannot help it. These things are so glaring to my sensitivities. However, I must admit that there are some good things even in those tabloids which seem to specialise in the sensational. They do have human stories that give encouragement and do tell of some of the good things that humans do. Occasionally, they have reports of human triumph over disasters, acts of selfless bravery and heartwarming accounts of patient endurance and fortitude. These, at least to me, are welcome. But the general contents of the popular newspapers are mostly concerned with the sensational and the scandalous. I am not sure this can be for the general good or the achievement of human happiness or contentment. But who am I to judge such things?

Perhaps I should add one further comment on my impression of these popular tabloids. They are written in a very simplistic style with short paragraphs and brief sentences. They are easy to read and make little demand on the intellectual capacity of the human reader. Sometimes I wonder what overall effect these newspapers must have on their readers. Perhaps they have their minds filled with tiny snippets of reality with no basic philosophy or theology into which they can be fitted. But, as I do not belong here, how can I understand the ways of the human creature?

I have heard of an early newspaper owner who had a card printed and put in the offices of his editors. The card read, 'Remember they are only ten.' This was to remind his editors continually of the mental age of his readers - only ten years. I suspect that they continue to regard their readers as little more than children who must be amused or excited as the only way of keeping their attention. Is that not a sad comment? If earthling children are always treated as children how can they ever become adults? I am bewildered as to how such things can be.

I can only bid you another sad farewell as I long to be where the Creator, and all his good gifts, are appreciated and enjoyed. I do not like it here where he seems to be forgotten and his gifts corrupted.

But, as always, I wish you peace and harmony.

Magazines for Leisure

Shamar to Pzylon: Earth Report 14

A hasty greeting. Immediately after I sent you my report on the newspapers it occured to me that I should have added a post script concerning the other popular reading material here. Hence this quick and rather brief report.

I should have pointed out that newspapers are not the only regular reading in this place. There are magazines which come out weekly or monthly. They are usually thicker and more colourful than newspapers and cover, with words and pictures, a bewilderingly vast array of subjects. In fact, it would be easily possible to go through the English alphabet by listing the magazines available. They contain every subject from A to Z, from advertising to zoology.

On the shelves of the newsellers here it is possible to find magazines dedicated to the following topics: Adventure; Art; Accounting; Books; Birds; Computers; Decorating; Drama; Dance; Education; Films; Gardening; Humour; Industry; Knowledge; Management; Music; Nature; Opera; Photography; Romance; Science; Sport; Television; UFO's (Unidentified Flying Objects); Videos; Wildlife; Yachting and Zoology. While this may seem to be comprehensive it really is only part of the variety available. Please, Pzylon, I know your sense of humour, do not ask me to report on all these subjects!

My first impression when I saw rows of magazines available was surprise as to how specialized they seemed to be. Perhaps this should not have surprised me as it is apparent that this is an age of specialization here. There was a time when an earthling male or female could be a philosopher, a poet, an artist or a scientist with a wide knowledge of many other subjects. That has gone. Intellectuals now acquire more and more learning about narrower fields of knowledge with little awareness of what is happening in other spheres of scholarship. This has spread to the common people. Therefore popular magazines are written and illustrated for special areas of interest.

With the explosion of the humans' knowledge in this century I can understand this development but, in some strange way, this both encourages me and disheartens me. My reactions are difficult to express.

The variety of specialized magazines obviously caters for a need. It shows that these human creatures have a wide range of interests and abilities. We know the Creator made all his creatures to be different, with diverse interests which can be united for the good of all the community. Popular magazines certainly reflect this diverse interest.

But I cannot see how it could have been the intention of the Creator, or for the good of human creatures, that a narrow specialization should prevail. It cannot be for the good when individuals have no interest or curiosity about other subjects than their own. When they make their own language and jargon they can no longer communicate with one another and problems must arise.

Such are the confusing thoughts that arise in me as I consider the popular magazines of this sad place. Most cater for one particular interest and nothing else. Few, if any, deal with the many facets of life on this planet. As I have written, I have found this strange for surely the Creator has given these creatures an innate curiosity about everything?

I have reported on the emphasis on sex which these human creatures seem to reveal in so many ways. Magazines are no exception. There are many magazines which seem designed to inflame sexual lust. They are called 'girlie magazines' and they specialize in detailed photographs of nude females for the titillation of males. Some even show sexual acts. I found this a sickening form of specialization. The Creator has given these human creatures the most personal and intimate form of relationship and this is being used by some magazines as a public show. Beauty and tenderness are often corrupted in this place. I find it all beyond my understanding.

There is one other form of magazine which I should mention - which I will boldly refer to as women's magazines. A large proportion of the magazines published here are designed for, and aimed at, women. Probably these should have a long detailed report but I will content myself with only a few observations.

They contain much that would be expected. Romantic stories which show the earthling females are more open to the concept of tender love and commitment, or at least this is my immediate impression. As the female human creature is generally seen as the home-maker there are lots of items dealing with this aspect of family life. There are pages with recipes for cooking and baking, home furnishing, child rearing and human relationships. Personal beauty seems always to be an important subject but I find it difficult to appreciate as here beauty is considered to be the surface appearance. They seem to ignore the fact that the most lovely of their flowers may be poisonous. Beauty, as we know, is more than appearance.

With the emphasis on appearance, these women's magazines have many features on fashion and clothes. It seems to be very important that the female human creature dresses according to the dictates of current fashion which lays down colour and such things as the length of body covering that may be worn. I must confess I do not know who exactly dictates these fashion changes but I suspect that it is the manufacturers who want to keep selling.

There are also many articles in these magazines revealing different kinds of diets. Being fat seems to be a horror here so there are many hints on how to lose weight. This fact, and all the other features I have mentioned, does reveal something of the earthling's culture. I have no doubt it would repay studying but I am here only to observe and report. Again I will leave such studies to those more able to pursue them than I am.

I must mention one more feature. All these magazines have an 'Advice Page' written by someone commonly referred to as 'Agony Aunt'. I understand that this is one of the most popular pages in many magazines. It has a staple format. Earthlings write in with their problems, their letter is published and advice given. In some magazines the advice seems sane and sensible but in others there seems to be no reference to any moral law. But I must confess that this page tended to sadden me beyond words.

I was pained on three accounts. Firstly, there was the

variety of problems which earthlings face. Although most of the letters were from women, some male creatures also wrote seeking helpful advice. There are so many worries and troubles in this place. I find it frightening how these humans hurt themselves and one another. This may be a place of glory but it is shot through with pain and it does not ease the suffering to know it is self-inflicted. I read these letters with sorrow and some almost brought tears to my eyes.

Secondly, I was sad to think that these creatures, in their problems and anxieties, had no one to whom they could turn. They had to write to a stranger for help. What has happened to human community where people help, support and encourage one another? There certainly is a lot of loneliness here.

Thirdly, and this was the most painful fact of all, in the problems and in the advice given, the Creator was never mentioned. I found this incomprehensible. No human ever seemed to suggest that the Creator would or could help. It was as if the Creator has no interest in his creatures, that he abandons them in their time of trouble. Have they ever heard of his love and power? Have they never heard of his compassion and pity? Apparently not. So he is ignored. Such things are beyond my understanding. Surely their own hearts can teach them to pray?

I meant this report, beloved Pzylon, to be a brief note but, perhaps as always, impressions crowd in on me and the words flow. But I do think we can learn much about this place from the magazines these human creatures read. I have only given some preliminary observations which can do little more than introduce the subject. You will, I know, forgive me if I have again failed your expectations.

Human and Important

Greetings. Sometimes I simply do not know what to make of these human creatures. They continue to surprise me in so many ways. Let me report on my latest surprise.

I saw a number of earthling women standing at the entrance of a building watching a wedding party emerge. A young woman came up and asked an older woman, 'Is it somebody important getting married?' 'No,' replied the older woman, 'It's just the girl who works in the supermarket over there.' The young woman then hurried on, apparently satisfied she was not missing anything.

I found the incident depressing. Perhaps, considering earthling culture, the answer of the old woman was understandable. The wedding party did not have any TV personalities, pop stars, famous athletes or politicians. It was only a girl who works in a supermarket. But how could she be considered unimportant?

Certainly that young bride must have been important to her parents. After all they had nurtured her all the days of her life. She must have been important to her proud-looking new husband who had just promised to love and cherish her until the marriage bond would be fractured by the cruel hand of death. Then, supremely, as we know, she is important to the Creator who made her, loves her and longs for her to live a real life.

But there are those who think she is nobody important - 'just a girl who works in the supermarket.' Sometimes I think that all these human creatures have unstable mental processes. However, it is not for me to judge.

The thought of this young bride who works in a supermarket has brought to my mind the practice of shopping here. I do not think I have reported on this aspect of human activity which is important for earthling mothers and wives and, indeed, for an increasing number of their men. Economic reasons have dictated that shops should get larger and larger so that bulk buying of goods leads to cheaper selling prices. Money is supremely important in this culture as I must have mentioned in earlier reports. So, for economic reasons, most shopping is done in supermarkets.

As the name suggests, supermarkets are large, sometimes huge, market places with corridor after coridor of shelves bearing every possible brand of groceries and household goods. The range on display is enormous and, at least to me, bewildering. I wonder how these human creatures can cope with the wide variety of goods on offer. In one small corner I counted forty different kinds of paste to clean teeth and fifty-one different brands of soap to clean the body! Even the necessities of life such as bread and drinks seem to have an almost infinite variety on offer which must confuse the customer as to which is best.

The supermarket is a sort of temple to consumerism, a cave of temptations. On entering, the customer takes a mobile container and is then involved in a conveyor belt type of shopping. She walks up and down the corridors of shelves selecting the goods she needs - and often the goods she does not need. These are laid out in tempting displays with multicoloured flash cards designed to catch the eye and encourage impulsive buying. Even the typography is suggestive; narrow letters describe a slimming drink; bright and bold letters advertise a powerful, dynamic detergent. Often music is played quietly in the background, not only lulling the customers into a genial mood, but creating pleasant feelings in weary breasts. The aim, I suspect, is to try to make buying more than is needed a pleasing experience. Occasionally the music is switched off and announcements are made from a breathless voice about unrepeatable bargains for the discerning shopper.

On completion of her shopping, the earthling customer goes to the checkout where the purchases are totalled on a calculating machine. The human who does this has no time to make conversation or to react like a human creature dealing with another human. The whole system seems to me to be completely soulless and very lonely. I do not know how these human creatures can do this sort of thing regularly.

It means that an earthling woman can leave her home, do all the shopping, and return home without actually speaking to another living soul. I find this idea sad and depressing. Surely the good Creator did not mean his human creatures to live like this?

Should not buying and selling, transacting business, be a human activity rather than a mechanical process? People are not robotic automatons, but sometimes in earthling culture they seem to be treated that way.

Beyond the checkouts there is an area with shelves where customers can load their goods from the metal containers into their own carrier bags or boxes. I have observed them - men, women and children - and always they seem to be preoccupied and harassed, almost burdened-looking. They seem to have no smiles or laughter. Such sights make my spirit heavy and sad. Should not the gathering of food for the earthling family home be a joyful and happy activity?

I believe these human creatures were made for one another and need to talk to one another. They are not economic robots gliding obediently along the shelves, responding to the tempting bargains on offer or moving quickly to the announced 'special offers'. I saw a delightful example of human behaviour which illustrates this perfectly.

A group of old women at the entrance to one of the corriders immediately started a conversation. One of them had recently been in hospital and was relating an amusing experience that had happened to her there. Soon there were gales of laughter and others remembered, and told, of the funny things that had happened to them. But these old ladies, happy to be together and sharing their experiences, were blocking the pathway for other shoppers. The anxious manager came to ask them to move on but they tried to bring him into their happy conversation.

I was on the side of those old ladies. Perhaps, from the manager's point of view, it was not good for business but I believe that it was a very human thing to talk, communicate and laugh together. But supermarkets are not designed for such activities as old ladies enjoying sharing experiences together. So they had to move on. Perhaps I should add that I saw them later, out in the street, happily continuing their conversation.

Incidents like that bring comfort to my heart. The Creator made these creatures to be human. As always, I wish you peace and harmony.

Books and Heroes

Greetings and again I accept your rebukes. I am sorry that you are disappointed at my 'wordy wanderings' as you call it. Perhaps I should be more organised but I tend simply to report on what strikes me as important rather than be systematic in my observations. This problem is compounded by the fact that I am always being bombarded by so many things in this place that, at times, I feel completely overwhelmed. As I seem endlessly to be repeating - I do not like this place.

Having received my reports on the human creature's newspapers and magazines you ask about books. I should have thought of them and can only ask your forgiveness for my continuously failing in my duties. In asking for your pardon I am comforted by the knowledge that it will be freely given. I know your graciousness, beloved Pzylon.

Now, about books. There can be no doubt these human creatures love stories. Whilst still in childhood they like stories about fairies and mythical creatures in some never-never land. This love does not leave them in adulthood or old age. Almost all like telling and listening to stories and anecdotes. It seems to me that this love of stories is part of being an earthling and is a valued gift of the Creator.

Although, in this place at this time, it seems to be

the age of television, pictures, symbols and signs, there are still many books on offer that are obviously read. I am not sure how widely. There seemed to be a time when there were bookshops in every main thoroughfare but these have been replaced by video hire shops. I suspect most humans now like their stories told by television. However, books have not departed from this planet.

In general, fictional stories are published as 'novels' and can be divided into two classes - literary works and popular paperbacks. It is no part of my duty to develop serious literary criticism so I can only make some general observations.

Serious novels, which are considered literary, are usually reviewed in literary magazines and quality newspapers. These are the sort of stories which try to illumine the human condition, explore emotional and intellectual life, and attempt to help the reader appreciate what it means to be a human being. While some of these books may be influential, I suspect that reading them is a minority interest. Such literary explorations of humanness are, of course, timeless and this means that many such writers of the past are still relevant. I should add that few of the so-called serious books published today really illumine human life to any great degree. I suspect that most will be quickly forgotten by the earthlings.

Popular books do not claim to examine or seriously explore the human dilemmas and are about action rather than personality. They offer an illusion, not an enrichment, of life and are read for relaxation.

As life in this place is often hard and monotonous, I do not think such escapist reading is necessarily wrong. It must be refreshing to human minds to escape for a few short hours into an imaginary world where all problems are solved and all difficulties overcome. But, I suspect, it cannot be for their good if human creatures read nothing but escapist literature.

It is on this area of popular books that I want to concentrate in this report. As in so much else in this place, the choice is bewildering.

To go into a bookshop is to be confronted with crowded shelves of card-covered manuscripts which are colourful and eye-catching. Many of the covers are lurid with images of sexuality and violence. Perhaps this also shows something of earthling culture. There is a wide variety of different types of stories within these covers - love stories, family sagas, thrillers, science fiction, mysteries and tales of horror. I need hardly add that I have no time to go into a detailed critique of all these themes.

Love stories, usually classified as 'romance' are very popular and sell by the millions. As may be expected it is usually the females of the species who buy and read these books. These romances are stories with a set pattern. A human woman and a man fall in love and, due to a misunderstanding or uncontrollable circumstance they separate. Eventually, however, all problems are resolved and they come together at the end to be married and live happily ever after.

There are many variations of this basic plot and, for added interest, the stories are often set in what are considered to be exotic countries or glamorous periods of history. The heroines and heroes are usually portrayed as chaste and loyal and act honourably in all that they do.

I confess that I am in two minds about these stories.

They tend to glorify earthling love as a purely emotional experience which must lead to life long happiness and this may raise false expectations. Love is more than mere emotion. But can I blame any human woman for wanting to lose herself in a world where true love triumphs over all difficulties and marriage means happiness ever after?

Of course, there are also corruptions of these love stories - sadly it seems there is nothing these human creatures cannot corrupt. Some books, masquerading as love stories, seem to me to be little more than an exultation of lust, with pages devoted to the physical details of sexual encounters given in graphic and sensational detail. In these books sexuality is presented as a force which tramples over such concepts as chastity, honour and faithfulness.

'Thrillers' are books which seem to be packaged and sold like soap powders with extensive advertising. They are heralded as 'blockbusters' - the meaning of which I have yet to determine. In these stories the reader is cast into a world of spies, secret police, terrorist groups and all sorts of adventurers who avert wars, thwart international criminals or save the world. The heroes of such books are little more than fantasy figures who are kinds of supermen beyond good or evil. Their characteristics seem to be bravery, dedication to some cause, ruthlessness in pursuit of some object and the distorted conviction that the end always justifies the means .

These books have plenty of action. Violence is vividly described and death never comes peacefully. Often they are spiced with sexual encounters, sometimes as brutal as the death scenes. It all seems to be a celebration of lust without love, violence without pity and based in a cruel world of the bully boy where the most ruthless always win. It is those on the side of the supposed good who are portrayed as the toughest and most ruthless. Some of these books which I have read horrify me. I fear the effect on those earthlings who read nothing else.

Perhaps I should admit that I am writing about the worst of these books. Doubtless there are many which are comparatively harmless adventure stories but it is the dark side of human life that troubles me most and impresses itself into my heart. As one who has seen and enjoyed the best, I am saddened to be confronted with the worst.

The problem with all their novels is that they seem to present a one-dimensional world. They are all about events on the physical level and of course this is not wrong. The Creator made them physical creatures but these humans are more than bodies, they are living souls. As so many of them do not believe in the Creator, they can only see a hostile universe inhabited by fragile men. They act and tell stories as if there was nothing beyond. In almost all their stories there is apparently no Creator to make sense of their world or the future. Individual earthlings must struggle against one another, against the fates and an unknown, but fearful, future. This must emphasize the absence of hope in the human heart.

I have said that most fiction sees nothing beyond the physical but there is one kind of novel which does bring with it another dimension. There seems to be a great increase in stories of the occult.

These books, which are their old ghost stories writ large, are about the supernatural. They are all about demon possession, evil spirits taking control of humans or dwelling areas and wreaking havoc in the lives of ordinary earthling men, women and children. What I have found disturbing and astonishing in this sort of novel is that the supernatural is always displayed as the forces of depravity and the vilest evil. Evil spirits abound but there seem to be no good spirits ready to do battle with the bad. This, as you and I know, Pzylon, is neither right nor true.

What strange creatures these humans are! Imagine reading horror for amusement! Sometimes I think there is no way I can ever really understand them.

As I have said, many of these books are for those earthlings who want to retreat from reality. If this is done occasionally I suspect it is probably beneficial for these creatures. Although they may not acknowledge him, the Creator has given them the ability to imagine and fantasize and, perhaps, this is mentally refreshing for them. I know not.

In these stories the absence of the Creator means the absence of moral absolutes. Thus the race can be won by the one who cheats his way to the front and the battle by the most ruthless. Self-interest, self-pleasure and self-satisfaction appear to be the main aims of many popular fictional characters. I hesitate to call them heroes because I know what that word really means.

This is an area which troubles me. I suspect that the young humans, male and female, need heroes and heroines to whom they can look up to, admire and strive to copy. Where the hero or heroine is brave and honest, with strict rules of morality and justice, then their influence must be for the good. If they portray the virtues of love, compassion, honour, decency and goodness they are worthy of admiration and are good models for the young to imitate.

I have not found such heroes or heroines in the popular earthling novels. Perhaps I have been looking in the wrong books or not sensitive enough to understand fully what is happening here at this time. But I am forced to wonder if human society and culture is betraying the young earthlings by encouraging a new type of hero such as a pop singer or someone who is good at some sport, or a TV personality. It seems to be these sorts of humans who are treated as heroes.

Beloved Pzylon, I find it hard not to become sadly cynical in this place. You must think that I am continuously looking on the black side and becoming obsessed with the wrong rather than the right. If this is so, I can only ask your forgiveness. But it is hard not to become depressed here. Even the good is tainted. The earthling books I have read all seem to imply that morality, love, duty, loyalty, even simple patriotism, are all old-fashioned virtues. How can I understand such things? Surely it is beyond all comprehension?

All I can say in conclusion is that I love my homeland with a great love. How I long to be back there in the regions of light! But here I must stay and do my duty and be faithful to my calling.

As ever, beloved Pzylon, I wish you peace and harmony.

Art and Alienation

Greetings. Having reported briefly on popular literature I turn to the arts in general. Perhaps, after my meandering over many subjects, this shows that I am beginning to answer your pleas and become organised. I hope you appreciate it!

This is a strange place but there is much here to warm my heart in spite of its horrors. There is the glory and beauty I mentioned in my first report.

These human creatures are highly endowed with imagination, ability, inventiveness and artistic skill. They have the capacity to dream of things that never were and then, with heart and hand, make that dream a reality. Not only do they make things of practical use but they can devise objects of awesome beauty. The Creator has been lavish in his gifts to these creatures and artistic creativity must be among his richest gifts. They seem to me to be a real celebration of what it means to be the image bearer of the Creator.

Painting, sculpture, architecture, music, drama, literature and poetry are among the arts of these human creatures. These can, in a unique way, communicate with the human spirit, touch the heart, stimulate the mind, fire the imagination, enrich the spirit and bring joy to the emotions. I suspect that the arts are essential for these creatures to be truly human. I cannot imagine this world devoid of colour, music, poetry or story telling.

This place has a glorious heritage of artistic works which illumine creation and reveal the human condition with burning truth. Art is timeless and I have seen the arts of past ages and know they still have power to bring awe and wonder.

Obviously I cannot go into all the details of the paintings I have seen, music I have heard or the literature I have read. I can only give some general observations and, indeed, that is all I am expected to do.

I have stood before paintings which truly celebrate the glory of created things and reveal human reality. They show the beauty and horror as well as the pleasures and pains of being human in this place. Such pictures have deepened my understanding of what it means to be human on this strange planet.

I have found myself having the same response when I stood before some of the great sculptures of past generations of these earthlings. They made me realise afresh the delightful proportions and power of the human form. To see movement frozen in marble is an illuminating experience.

Architects have erected marvellous buildings which can only be described as awe-inspiring. They soar into the heavens revealing grandeur and glory. With carvings and stone tracery, turrets and towers, arched windows and richly decorated doors, they stand as practical monuments to the imagination and ability of the architects who built them.

There is also a glorious literary heritage. There are many novels which explore the great themes of earthling life and death and show, with truth and compassion, the human heart as a battleground of good and evil. My knowledge of humans has been enlarged by the reading of these books. Poetry also has enriched this culture. There are poems which sing of love and joy, as well as the disappointments and pains of the human experience. Others rejoice in the many splendours of creation, finding enchantment in unexpected places or seeing a radiance all around. Poetry can bring enchantment.

Allied to literary art is their drama. Many great earthling plays of the past are still relevant today and they can be, as one playwright suggested, 'a mirror to nature'. They can show the human heart in pursuit of love, vengeance, acceptance, status or any of the other emotions that drive these human creatures.

Then there is their music which my sensitivities demand that I describe as the most direct and emotive of all the arts. There are symphonies, oratorios, operas and songs expressing everything from ecstasy to mourning. Music certainly seems to move the earthling heart and touch their deepest emotions. It may be a fancy in my mind but I suspect that the best of their music is but an echo of the endless rejoicing to be found in the abode of the Creator.

So, beloved Pzylon, I have been impressed by the arts of these human creatures. They seem to me the highest and noblest expressions of human experience.

But what of the arts today? I have submitted myself to the earthlings' contemporary arts and I have to say it has been a most uncomfortable experience. Perhaps I am not fully acquainted with the mind set of these human creatures and am unable to know their emotional response but it does seem to me that confusion has replaced cultural enrichment and despair has taken over from delight.

In their modern art galleries I have wandered around with a growing sense of bewilderment and alienation.

Craft work seems to have disappeared and has been replaced by splattered canvasses, full of colours signifying nothing. The graceful lines of the old earthling sculptures have been superceded by shapeless stones, folded blankets, crushed cars, arrangements of bricks or piles of old scrap metal. I found it all depressing and cannot see how these things can enhance an earthling knowledge of reality and make them more aware of what it means to be human. They seem to portray a world from which form, meaning and beauty have departed and all that is left is an emotional response which is beyond rationality and understanding.

Of course, it may be that modern human art is not meant to point to anything beyond itself. Perhaps it is not intended to reveal a world of order and meaning, beauty and balance, and has become purely subjective, communicating nothing but an emotional response. If this is so then I find it sadly depressing.

I can say little about earthling architecture except that it is clear that economics are now more important than aesthetics. Grey concrete edifices are built with little in the way of decoration or beauty. They are utilitarian rather than artistic. Not surprisingly, many modern buildings are soulless and, at least to me, convey nothing of human greatness.

The same seems to be true of modern literature. Great novels examining the great themes of life seem to have gone. Many of their contemporary novels seem to suggest that seduction and sex are the great pursuits of human life. The anti-hero is treated as of more worth than the lone hero struggling to overcome all that can be thrown against him. The poetry of the age appears to be lacking rhyme, rhythm and reason. It requires study and mental effort to extract meaning from the jumble of words. I found it all wearisome.

In drama I found the sad corruption that covers so much here. In many ways blasphemy, nudity and simulated sex on stage, allied with the language of the gutter, are presented as public entertainment and aesthetic experience. Like popular novels, they seem to want to present sin without remorse and violence without pity. I find it both confusing and sad.

Modern earthling music comes to my ears as a babel of sounds without the grace of melody. At a popular level, the current musical taste is for a beat to thrill the body rather than to lift the human spirit. It all sounds a vexation to me.

This new art may however (and I think this must be the most plausible reason) be a reflection of how the humans see their own surroundings and their involvement in them. Their art therefore depicts the mechanism and materialism which the earthlings have developed for themselves. The brokenness and hopelessness which is conveyed is depressing but somehow it shows that the earthling recognizes at least that there is something wrong and broken about himself. The mere acknowledgement of this may lead to some change. What form this may take I have yet to observe or comprehend!

Although this reasoning may be correct, I do not like this place. The contemporary arts confirm my early impressions that these human creatures have lost their way and everything I have observed only seems to make more confusion abound. I may be wrong about this, perhaps I simply do not know what is happening here, but I do suspect that earthling arts increasingly are being removed from the majority of human creatures. They are being alienated from them.

My observations lead me to believe that most earthlings find that most contemporary expressions of their arts are obscure and beyond their understanding. To them modern art is a foreign language. It has its own secret syntax and speaks with strange symbols and imagery with no key for comprehension. Rather than being a source of inspiration to wonder and awe it is alienating common humanity from an important part of their creational inheritance. Rather than opening their eyes to the glories of creation it is seeking to drive them into their own private emotions. This cannot be for the good.

To me, if art does not point beyond itself, and help the viewer, listener or reader to look beyond the feelings of his own heart then it fails. I have only to look around to see that these human creatures were made to live in a world where there is much to please the eye for they are surrounded by beauty, order and glory. Should not the arts reflect this? Then there is truth, the rock of reality, on which these humans must live and struggle in a world gone mad. Truth must be something beyond the feelings of the heart or the emotions of the breast. Should not the arts reflect this and not merely the brutal fragmentation of values manufactured by man himself?

What troubles me is that the arts do exist but appear as if they are only for an elite who alone can appreciate the finer things of life. They are beset by pride and snobbishness as if the Creator had not given the gift of arts for the benefit of all his human creation. It should not require an extensive knowledge of the history of earthling art to appreciate a picture. It should not need a university degree in literature to understand a novel or poem and it should not involve a study of aesthetics for them to enjoy their music. But such things seem necessary here in this sad place.

Of course, there is a popular culture. Human creatures need music, poetry, stories and pictures to remain truly human. But it saddens me with an infinite sadness to see what is happening in the sphere of the arts. What was once known as the 'Fine Arts' or 'High Art' now seems to be the preserve of the intellectual and snobbish few. It is not for all earthlings. How can it be when it is apparently beyond their common understanding?

In spite of the joy with which I began this report the now familiar greyness of depression is again descending on my spirit. How can it ever be otherwise in this place? Even my brief study of the earthling arts has shown me how they can help these people to be more human and lift their eyes to see that there is more to life than economic materialism and sociological understanding. But the arts have alienated themselves from the very creatures they are meant to serve. I fear there is a generation of earthlings deprived of dreams. How can I not find it sad?

Again I must close by expressing the pain I am experiencing as I observe this place and long to be back to where I belong, that place of beauty for which I was made. That pain is intensified by pity for these poor humans who try to find joy among the dark debris of a world gone wrong. Certainly the things I see and hear cannot be in the will of the Creator who is good. Tragically these people neither fear or worship him. Even some of their arts often seem a blasphemy against his name. However I know he has his own people here. I must report on them soon.

So with a renewed heavy heart and a sadness that invades all my being, I wish you which is in short supply here - peace and harmony.

Weary and Worried

Shamar to Pzylon: Earth Report 18

Greetings. Perhaps you are right as always. The pain of being here colours all my observations and may indeed, as you suggest, make me mostly see the dark side of this sad place. But it is not self-pity that governs my heart, but pity for these human creatures. They irritate me, bewilder me, even anger me, but as far as I know my own heart, I truly pity them. I can report an incident which illustrates what I mean.

I saw them sitting in a Doctor's waiting room: a man and a woman, each alone and locked in their own thoughts and misery. They did not know one another, so sat side by side not even acknowledging each other's existence. This seems to be a common characteristic here: humans who share the same planet, the same community, the same humanity, yet make no attempt to communicate with each other. Is that not strange?

But let me tell you about them so that the pity I feel will be in your own heart too, beloved Pzylon. It is a sad story.

She was a small woman, still young in years, perhaps no more than thirty years of human life. But there was a tiredness, almost bitterness, in the thin line of her lips and the frown ageing her features. Her eyes, once bright with the sheen of youth, were now dead, as if the light of life had been extinguished. Sitting with blank face and huddled shoulders, she portrayed a picture of fear, guilt and bitterness. Just by looking at her I knew her story. I gave my sensitivities free range.

There was no love for her husband in her heart for it had slowly withered away. She no longer had patience with her children and despaired of life ever improving. She faced the future with a sense of hopelessness and infinite weariness.

Perhaps her growing disillusionment with her husband was justified. Like so many men here he seemed to be deficient in his sense of responsibility to wife and children. Clubs, pubs (which are earthly gathering places sadly tainted by their primary function of supplying intoxicating drugs in liquid form) and the local football team dominated her husband's life and rather than spend time with his family he preferred, in his own words, 'to go out with the boys'. The children, sensing the tension between their parents, were growing wild and disobedient, striving to get attention and love from parents who no longer even seemed to respect one another. It was not a happy home.

There was also envy in the woman's heart. It was with something akin to pain that she thought of her sister, living in a large house in a residential part of the town with apparently all that life could offer. She had a loving husband, quiet and obedient children and no financial worries. They seemed to go everywhere as a family as if they all enjoyed being together.

So, cocooned in despairing self-pity and envy, the tired woman sat in the surgery waiting room and thought bitterly of how life had stolen all her early dreams. Now she was tired and weary as she numbly waited on the bell ringing to indicate that she could go and see the doctor.

Beside her sat the man, once quite handsome and

distinguished-looking, but now appearing worried and ill at ease. As far as years on this planet are concerned he had only fifty five, but his lined face and clouded eyes made his look almost like an old man.

He sat musing on how difficult it would be to explain to the doctor what exactly was wrong with him. There were the headaches of course, the dull pressure behind his eyes that made it hard to concentrate. Then there was the perpetual tiredness that had invaded his body, the difficulty in sleeping, lack of appetite, and the continual discomfort in his stomach. But he wondered if it was all in his mind. How could he explain to the doctor the intense sense of failure that now haunted his days and nights. It was as if although he was not dead, life had come to a sudden stop.

It had all happened so suddenly. He thought he was safely employed with a family business that had a secure future and then, without warning, it happened. The firm had gone bankrupt and his well-paid employment had come to an end. There had been no golden handshake in the form of a large amount of money to take the sting out of unemployment and so the debts remained.

Even in the quietness of the doctor's waiting room endless questions revolved around his mind. How could they live? How could they move from the beautiful bungalow they had bought only four years ago? But how could they afford the present payments? Would they have to give up the car and the foreign holiday they had already booked? How could he remain friends with those with whom he spent his leisure time, in his 'Bridge Club' and 'Golf Club' when the stigma of unemployment would be attached to his name? What would the future hold? How could he get another job at his age? He and his wife had always been used to easy living and plenty of money - there had never been any need to save.

His wife said little but he knew she blamed him. He was the breadwinner and he had often boasted that his wife had never needed to go out to work. Guiltily he felt the misfortune was all his responsibility. So he felt worried and helpless. It was his wife who moodily had suggested that he should go and see the doctor.

Both of them, the weary woman and the worried man, sat waiting in tense silence in the doctor's waiting room. Both vaguely felt that the doctor would be able to help. He would be able to give them something to ease the discomfort of weariness and banish the pain of worry.

Were they really looking for pharmaceutical salvation? Is that not bewilderingly sad?

In some ways these two unfortunate human creatures illustrate the human dilemma. With thoughts of a loving Creator gone from their minds they had nowhere beyond themselves, or other humans, to turn for help. They were in a frightening condition where help, as we know, was awaiting them but they had closed their eyes to the possibility of assistance from beyond their world.

Does not such a thing sadden your heart, beloved Pzylon? I find it almost incomprehensible that such things can be. But such things are in this place. After all, if there is no God, there is nothing - just lonely souls inhabiting a lonely planet. Morality and salvation must be human inventions and all human creatures can only struggle on in their own strength.

I can only pity these creatures with a great pity. So, once more with heavy heart, I wish you the things they lack - peace and harmony.

Gods and Idols

Greetings and, as always, you are right. It is time for me to look at what the Creator has done for this spoiled planet and observe something of his work amongst the people of the Prince. But first, I must tell you of a new thought which has come to my mind which has illuminated and transformed all my thinking. These human creatures are basically religious creatures.

Certainly, as I have clearly observed, they may not worship the great and good Creator who made all things, but they do serve and pay homage to many gods and idols. It is a strange phenomenon. They see creation but do not ackowledge the Creator. They study the laws of nature but do not believe in a Lawgiver. They appreciate the gifts men have but ignore the Giver. Instead, they have substituted idols and strange gods for their works of worship. With hearts, souls, minds and bodies they serve these idols of their own devising. I can only list some of these strange gods and idols.

Art

As I have reported, art is wonderful expression of the creativity of human creaturehood and is undoubtedly a rich gift from the Creator. But art can and has, been made into an idol - a select and elitest idol.

The adherents to this idol have culturally-sacred

temples called art galleries which must be entered with reverent quietness. They also have many meeting places in the form of theatres, concert halls, opera houses and cinemas where cultural presentations are made for the edification of the devout.

The prophets, priests and kings of this idol are often seen as being above all moral laws and restraints. The religion of art gives artists total freedom in all that they want, do or say. 'Censorship' is the only blasphemous word in their liturgy and, strangely, although they believe the arts can inspire and refine, they deny they can corrupt or degrade.

Art, as an idol, offers cultural salvation because aesthetic appreciation is the begining of all wisdom, so they believe. Alone, their art can be the true source of revelation bringing redemption to the alienated and lost.

Music

Music is another good gift from the Creator which many earthlings have turned into an idol or surrogate god. Many, particularly the young, worship the idol of pop music with an intense reverence and their devotion often seems total.

Adherents love to gather together at great pop concerts or rock festivals to have communal acts of worship and fellowship. There they can shout their incantations and dance to the mortal music makers who are treated as immortals.

The devotees of this music god have many icons in the shape of emblems, clothing and pictures to turn their bedrooms into shrines. They buy recordings of the music makers so that they can listen to their confessions of faith over and over again and often carry transistors so that they need never be deprived of the music which is the sustaining spirit of their religion. It is with that music they want to live and breathe.

Sport

Sport and physical exercise are also among the good gifts of the Creator to these humans but many have turned them into false gods. They are a multi-faced idol. Their rituals are performed by a select few who live dedicated, almost monastic, lives of rigorous training and purification. They run, jump, swim, ride, fight, wrestle and play games as individuals or in teams.

International festivals of sport are held regularly which are full of religious symbolism and liturgies. Flags are carried, torches lit, hymns sung, oaths taken and ceremonial presentations of laurel wreaths or medals are made to the winners.

The devotees of these idols love to gather in large, open air cathedrals named football, cricket, racing, athletic or sports grounds. There they can offer praise and adoration to those taking part in such events by hymns of praise and prayers for victory and the defeat of sporting enemies.

Sport is an idol which offers excitement, vicarious thrills and the opportunity of transcendent experience which thrills the heart. Many see this idol as the true source of abundant life.

Money

The ancient god, mammon, seems to be alive and well in this place. Indeed, the accumulation of wealth is amongst the most popular idol of the age. Many, of all ages, are prepared to dedicate health and strength to serve the false god of money.

The basic creed of this faith is that true life consists of

having an abundance of possessions. Its worshippers have an almost mystic belief in the life-giving properties of money which alone can give security and salvation. They believe it is from wealth that all blessings flow.

Politics

Politics is a necessary activity in this place but many have turned it into an idol. It does have many devoted and dedicated servants. They sing the praise of some ideology and love to magnify a particular political system. Their voices are often raised in adoration of economic and political manifestos which, they believe, will lead mankind into a promised land of peace and prosperity.

It is another multi-faced idol with many denominations and sects. Although they may hate one another with almost a perfect hatred they have one thing in common, for they believe that man, unaided by any other god, will create a perfect society. Then there will be no more pain or sorrow and justice will cover the Earth.

Science

Science, as I understand it, is the earthling response to the Creator's mandate to rule and open up the riches of creation. But many have made it an idol and the only source of truth.

Those who worship at the shrine of science believe it is the god who will reveal all mysteries and save humanity from all sins. Science, and her only begotten son, Technology, are seen by their devotees as the gods who will subdue the earth and conquer the heavens so that, at the end, all things will be under the dominion of men. There is faith that science will abolish all pain, poverty, disease and death from the face of this Earth and then technological salvation will spread throughout the universe. To some science alone is the ultimate truth and guide in life.

Nature

As I think I have previously reported, 'Nature' is the word used by these human creatures to describe creation. But, as they have pushed the idea of a Creator from their minds, many have turned the creation into an idol.

'Nature' is seen by its devotees as an autonomous god, having her own laws and creative powers. Her worshippers see her as a mother god who gently rules over all and is the driving force of the strange doctrine which they call 'evolution'. Their poets have often sung hymns to 'Nature' believing her the god who soothes all pains, brings comfort to the broken-hearted, solace to the sorrowful and freely bestows her blessings on all humankind. She is seen as a bountiful god.

I must confess that I do not fully understand all the doctrines of this faith as those who pay homage to 'Nature' often reveal a curious scale of values. At times they appear to have more concern and compassion for trees, wild flowers, seals, whales and elephants than for human beings. In an age of the mass killing of unborn babies through abortion, the growing practice of infanticide and increasing pressure for euthanasia, those devoted to Nature seem to have little to say about such things. I find it all so very confusing.

But to them Nature is seen as wonderful, a comforting counsellor, a mighty god and the provider of peace. She is believed to reign in power and glory.

Art, music, sport, money, politics, science and nature are but a few of the strange gods and idols served in this sad place. But in reality their name is legion. There is nationalism, racism, rationalism, humanism, hedonism, business, economics and education, to say nothing of the many strange forms of mysticism such as astrology and the occult. It is all beyond my understanding. These human creatures seem to believe anything, and trust anything, rather than the Creator who made them. Their minds seem to be capable of manufacturing endless idols.

I find it contradictory and confusing. All these things which I have listed as idols are innocent in themselves, indeed they are good gifts given for human use and benefit. So they must be of great value when used aright. But many of these human creaures have taken these things, made them into an end in themselves, and so turned them into idols to be served and adored.

I hope you can understand what I am trying to say, beloved Pzylon. I am not sure I can understand it myself and can only wonder that such things can be. These humans seem to be either blindly stupid or stupidly blind. I know not which. I write these things not in arrogant pride but with pity in my heart.

If it is not sacrilege, I find myself actually feeling pity for the good and great Creator. He made these creatures, giving them so many gifts and abilities, and yet they deliberately use these talents to ignore or even deny him. How it must pain his heart of love.

Then, of course, I pity with a great compassion these human creatures. They could all live lives full of peace, love and joy if only they turned to the Giver of all their gifts. But they will not. I can see now what earlier merely bewildered me: now I am merely saddened. They would rather depend upon their own strength and go their own way even although the end is darkness.

Sadly, I must confess, I am touched with self-pity. I have known what it is to live joyously in a real world where the Creator is acknowledged, loved and obeyed. I know the glory of such a life. And here I am in such a place as this! It pains my heart as I yearn for the peace and harmony I have known.

But, I will obey my calling and do my duty. I wish you what I continually find lacking in this place - peace and harmony.

The Book of Books

Greetings from one whose heart has been warmed and whose spirit is soaring in wonder and praise. This is still a sad and pitiful place but I now know, in a way I have never known, the essential love and grace of the Creator.

As you know, beloved Pzylon, we have only heard echoes and hints of what the Creator has done in this planet. We have known of his love for these human creatures even in their rebellion against him. We know that he has had servants to tell of his ways and that the Young Prince of Glory actually visited this planet. I have now been learning of all these things and I can only stand in awe and amazement at his patience and grace which is infinite. Let me tell you about it.

He has done two things. He has given these human creatures a book which reveals himself and tells of the pathway which leads to eternal bliss. Then, even more startling, he has come into this planet - the Creator visited his creation in the form of a creature! Can anything be more wonderful, almost unimaginable, yet true?

But let me tell you of the book. I have spent many happy hours reading and re-reading this book which humans call the Bible. It is a remarkable book, indeed more than a book, it is a library of books, a book of books.

Rather than a philosophical or theological treatise, it is the sort of book which anyone can read with profit and interest. It contains historical narrative, biography, auto-biography, drama, poetry, parables, ethical teaching and much else. There are riches galore in its pages.

Even considered as a book it is an astonishing thing. It was written over a long period of time - centuries according to the human measurement of time. It has the style of many authors. But it has a harmonising unity because, behind every author, there is the mark of the supreme Author, the Creator God himself. He inspired the individual writers to reveal what he intended to say to all generations of human beings.

There is no way in which I could summarize the contents of this book of books. I can only try to give a brief outline.

It begins with creation. As a book of life it must begin with the creation of life. So when these humans deny the Creator they are doubly condemned, for creation all around proclaims the existence of a Creator and his book records the fact that 'In the beginning God made the heavens and the Earth.'

As we would expect (indeed, how could we expect otherwise?) it was a good creation. There was beauty and all that is necessary for life, with animals and birds, fish and fowl living together in perfect harmony in a beauteous creation which the Creator himself proclaimed to be 'very good'. The apex of creation was man - man made in the very image of God, made to be lord of creation, the Creator's steward over all things. How peaceful and harmonious that garden of creation must have been on that first dawn!

Now that fair garden lies in ruins with the beauty choked by weeds. Now, having read the book, I know what happened and what is really wrong in this place. It was simply this - man did not want to be subject to God. He wanted to go his own way, do his own thing and decide his own destiny. A stupid idea, as we know and humanity has discovered to its cost.

God gave man freedom and limitation, liberty and law, the perfect balance for all created things. But man rebelled against law and limitation and thought he could be a god. In this he was deceived by the Evil One, the enemy of the Most High, and is still as easily deceived.

So in the beginning man rebelled against God and plundered the garden of creation as if all things were his own. By this act he fell from his high estate of lord of all creation and the great divide entered the planet. Man found that enmity with God meant that he had become an enemy of his own good and his own kind. The brute creation in turn rebelled against man and the curse of God fell on the ground. The sickness of sin infected all things and entered into man's very being so that it became part of the human race.

Now I see what really is happening here and what sort of place this planet really is - it is a fallen world inhabited by fallen humanity. Yet earthling men and women still retain some of their original glory and their world still echoes something of its pristine beauty.

Here can be seen the wondrous grace of the Creator. He did not destroy these rebellious creatures or leave them helpless in their sin and sorrows. He still loved these humans who did not love him. So, right from the beginning of their rebellion, he promised redemption. He also promised the Evil One would be crushed and righteousness and right living would be rewarded.

The book tells of how God chose a man and a people who would be his own particular race of men. They would learn of his love and ways and would take this knowledge to all the peoples of the world. They would be a light and an example to all.

Much of the book is taken up with the history of these chosen people and the hard lessons they had to learn because of their disobedience. They found themselves helpless slaves in another country called Egypt. 'Slaves' I know will shock you. They are , I believe, humans who are bought by other earthlings for money who thereafter own them and force them to work on their behalf! This is the horrid condition brought about by the humans craving for possessions. But with great wonders and signs their God rescued them and took them to a land where peace and prosperity awaited them. But even on the journey they grumbled and complained, continually finding fault with the God who had done so much for them. (I must add that this is more than mere history. I find here that many earthlings, on their journey of life, still readily complain and accuse God of all the misfortunes they bring upon themselves.)

It was while the chosen people were travelling to their promised land that God revealed himself as the Lawgiver. It was a law not only for his own people but for all mankind of all the ages.

It was a good law containing ten points. They had to acknowledge God, have no false gods and treat the Almighty's name with reverence. One day in seven was to be set aside as God's special, holy day. They had to honour their parents, not kill, and to respect their marriage vows. Also, they had not to steal, lie or covet what did not belong to them.

Are these not good laws for earthlings and their

communities to live by? Would it not make happy lives and harmonious cities and peoples? But this good book keeps reminding the reader of how God's chosen race kept forgetting and ignoring this law. There seemed to be a spirit of that lawlessness in their very souls that is still evident. The sickness of sin is deep-rooted.

Wilful disobedience seems to be the hallmark of earthlings, and of God's people, as recorded in the book. In his grace and compassion, the Creator kept sending messengers - prophets to warn the lawless and bring them back to himself and the ways which led to peace. But they would not. They killed the prophets and murdered those who were sent. In the accounts of these events two things shine through. Firstly, there were those who were faithful men and women who humbly trusted their God, loved mercy and walked in his ways. They shine like dazzling beacons on a dark night and their lives were living proof that God's grace can come in to a human heart. These faithful ones must have been dear to God's heart. Certainly the sad world was not worthy of them.

The second strand in the book to shine through is the bright assurance that God would not be defeated. His witnesses may fail but God would not let his creation perish whilst something else could be done. So he promised, time after time, to come to the rescue himself. He would gather the lost sheep, he would bind up the wounded, bring good news to the downhearted, freedom to the prisoners of inherited sin and proclaim the time of God's free grace. And it came to pass.

The Creator sent his own Son, the Prince of Glory. This means as we know, dear Pzylon, that he came himself. He came to this sad planet and took the name of Jesus. I will report on this visitation later. It is a story more exciting than anything else in all history of all the worlds. Here I will only say, he came and he was rejected, but some humans believed. They then had the right to become children of God - what a glorious privilege! Men with wicked hands killed him but he rose again from the dead and became the way, the truth and the life for all who humbly believe.

The story of this matchless life is contained in four little books in the Good Book. The remainder of the Book of books is concerned with the good news of the Prince spreading throughout the world, and letters of teaching, exhortations and advice about how to live as his followers in a fallen world.

Then the Good Book ends with a vivid, pictorial account of dramatic batttles that will be fought between the Evil One and the sovereign God. It comforts with the assurance that nothing, and no one, can defeat the One who rules over all. Then, in the end, the Prince himself will return in glory with all the holy celestial beings. There will be a new Heaven and a new Earth. All that was lost in the vanished Eden and more, will be restored and the plagues of this fallen world will be no more - no death, no sorrow, no tears, and no sin. All will be made anew and the People of the Prince will be welcomed into the place their Lord has prepared for them. It is a thrilling story.

All this, beloved Pzylon, is but the briefest sketch of the riches of the Book of books. I have not touched on its many facts which deal with human relationships one with another as well as with God. There is wisdom for everyday living. There is poetry which can lift the heart to heaven with words expressing the deepest emotions. There are stories that can lift the burdened heart with hope and joy, and others which bring tears to the sensitive eyes. I do not see how any earthling could tire of reading the pages of the Good Book. It speaks to every heart and every possible human condition and contains the Creator's guide for his creation.

This book is freely available here but, sad to say, it seems to be largely ignored by most humans. I find myself wondering if even the followers of the Prince value it as much as they should or if they read and hide its riches in their hearts. I know not and it is not for me to judge. I am here simply to observe.

Others, of course, not only refuse to read it, but refuse to believe it. Rather than seeing it as the Word of God they treat it as myths, legends, fairy tales and merely the work of imaginative men. I can only pity such blindness. They are losing much in this life and losing even more in the life to come.

This Book of books has certainly lifted my heart and cheered my soul. The Creator has not deserted this place but, with loving heart, is still appealing for his rebellious human creatures to come back to him and live. And the Prince, who walked the dusty roads of this planet long ago is still, through his words in the Book appealing to men and women, young and old, to come and follow him. He offers forgiveness and peace to all. But more of that later.

Peace and harmony to you, beloved Pzylon.

The Prince and the Parties

Greetings from your observer who is now not so cheerful. I had intended to report on the earthly life of the Prince as recorded in the Book of books, but I find myself witnessing events which both confuse and depress me.

It is 'Christmas' here, a word the earthlings use to celebrate the coming of the Prince of Glory into this dark world. When I first heard about it, my heart leapt with joy. This was truly something to commemorate with rejoicings. Sadly, I found the reality mystifying.

Christmas is a remarkable phenomenon. It seems to be a time for children, for families and, indeed, for all the earthling community. It is a time of festivities, feasting, merry-making, and the giving of gifts with a warm spirit of goodwill. All this seems to be for the good. As we know, beloved Pzylon, individual, family and communal celebrations enrich life and are a joyous part of creaturehood. But I am bewildered at what is happening here at this season of Christmas.

My perplexity can be easily stated - if Christmas is a communal birthday party for the Prince of Glory, why does he have so little part in it? It seems to be a wonderful party where the guest of honour is ignored. I find it all so very peculiar.

Certainly it is a happy celebration with gaily-coloured decorations in homes, offices, factories and even on the streets. Multi-coloured lights are strung along the streets of the cities and shop windows are aglow with warmth and colour. Fir trees, renamed Christmas trees for the season, are in homes and public squares, festooned with little lights, glittering strips of foil, coloured baubles and a doll on top. (This doll, which has little wings and wears a long dress, is what most humans believe an angel looks like! I need hardly tell you, Pzylon, it is a poor imitation of an angel!)

All this helps to create a spirit of good cheer and joy which is good but, of course, it is also seen as having a commercial value. So the merchants and admen take advantage of this time by persuading everyone that this time of giving and love can only be truly expressed by the presentation of gifts.

Strangely, at least to my understanding, the symbol of this giving is not the Young Prince who gave up glory for this dark Earth, but a vaguely mystical figure called 'Father Christmas' or 'Santa Claus'. He is a mythical man who comes to each home in the early hours of Christmas morning to leave gifts for the children. Of course, these gifts are left by the parents who are pressurised to shower (I would say burden) their children with presents.

This donation of presents extends far beyond the earthling children and there are many exchanges of gifts within families and friends. Many who have little of Earth's wealth will find it a very expensive and worrying time as it is commonly assumed that the giving of gifts is the only way to express love. As if love could be measured in material things!

Not only presents are exchanged but millions of decorative communications are sent during this festive season. I found it interesting, and rather confusing, to study the designs on these coloured cards. The images and symbols on these cards seem to have little to do with the Prince. It is almost as if they had plundered the pagan religions of the Earth's past to find designs suitable for the Christmas celebrations. So they have yule logs burning and various other emblematic plants from the botanic sphere: mistletoe, holly and gaily-decorated trees. They have humanized animals, candles and red-breasted birds on snowy trees. Some show drawings of a supposed golden age with family round a blazing log fire, carol-singing outside an old house, or the interior of an old inn with men in ancient dress drinking a toast. On others there are romantic images of horse-drawn transport from another era of this society racing through a snow-clad landscape. Many of these cards are quite artistically designed but, to me, they seem to have nothing to do with the Prince whose birthday it is supposed to be.

Of course, I should mention that some cards do try to convey something of what the festival really means. I have seen Christmas cards with stable scenes and images of the birth of the Prince on Earth. But such cards are in the minority.

Christmas appears also to be a time of great feasting. With families and friends there is no end to the parties that are held, where there is plenty eating and drinking. I suppose these really should be called 'birthday parties' except for the sad fact that the One whose birthday they are supposed to be celebrating is rarely invited. I doubt if he would be welcomed!

As you will see, beloved Pzylon, the whole thing completely bewilders me. I do not quite know what to make of it all. Should I welcome it or condemn it? Even as an observer I find, at times, I have to take sides in the way I report events.

Some good probably comes out of this season. Human creatures are apparently more generous at this time of their year so perhaps something of the Prince's teaching still has influence. Charities are remembered and there is much selfless giving to those who are in need.

I can only suggest that others, with more intelligence and insight than I have been given, should analyze what happens to these human creatures at this time of Christmas. I have been giving the matter some thought and find myself wondering if there are three things all muddled up in this Christmas festival.

There seems to be a sort of midwinter festival taking place. Christmas here comes at the turn of the winter season when the darkest nights are beginning to go and the slowly-lengthening days bring the promise of spring and summer.

Secondly, there seems to be what I can only describe as a 'celebration of consumerism' taking place. In a materialistic culture it is things which are important and the buying and getting of more and more things is seen as the only path to satisfaction and fulfilment.

Thirdly, there are a few humans (I fear they are few but I know not) who genuinely celebrate with humble adoration the coming into the world of the Prince of Glory. It rejoices their hearts to remind themselves that at a certain point in history, at a certain place in this dark world, the Prince came.

Perhaps these are little more than guesses as to what is happening here this Christmas. I know not. As in so much else in this sad place I find myself bemused.

Enough for now. I will report next on the real coming of the Prince into this fallen world.

God and Man

Greetings. Now I come back to the promised report of the coming of the Prince into this sad and strange world. It is the most beautiful of all stories, bright with love yet tinged with tragedy, but the happiest of all endings. What makes it such a lovely story is not that the plot ends happily but that all creatures can live happily as a result.

In many ways it is an incredible story - that the Creator should become a creature in his own creation. But we know that just because something is beyond our understanding is no argument for saying it did not happen. It did happen. God became a man.

The Prince of Glory was not born in the vicinity in which I find myself but was born amongst God's chosen people, Israel, in their own land. Of course, he did not enter the world in the same manner as these mortal humans. A virgin, by the name of Mary, was told by an angel of God that she would bear a son. The man to whom she was engaged to be married, Joseph, also had an angelic visitor who told him of what was to happen and that he was to call the child's name 'Jesus', as that is the word for 'Saviour' in the Israelites language. This was the sign that he would save his people from their sins.

In response to the edict of the ruling authorities they

had to go to a dwelling place called Bethlehem to register in a taxation census. That little town was crowded and Mary and Joseph could only find shelter in a stable. It was there, among the lower beasts of creation that Jesus was born. That birth would affect all human creatures to the very ends of the Earth for all time but that little town of Bethlehem did not know - or care. But highest heaven was involved and all the angels sang at the glorious event they had witnessed.

Those earthlings whose hearts and minds are fixed on Earth neither see nor hear angels. On the occasion of the coming of the Prince, only some simple men called shepherds saw the angels and obeyed the heavenly messengers by going to Bethlehem to see this baby who would transform all things. Later, some rich in wisdom travelled from afar to worship the Prince who was born to be King.

Then the Evil One, who hates with a fiercesome hatred the Creator and all his works, made his first attack. Joseph, Mary and the baby had to flee from Israel and find refuge in Egypt, that eastern land of which I reported previously. Herod, an evil earthly ruler, had wanted to kill the new-born King. Such wickedness seems always to have been rampant on this planet.

But Herod went the way of all humanity, dying and finding himself before the Judge of all. Joseph brought Mary and the child Jesus back to his home town of Nazareth. There for many years they seemed to live quietly and simply.

There is so much the human creatures would like to know about that home in Nazareth but the historical records of the Gospels give no information. Like the Good Book itself in which these Gospels appear they were not written to satisfy curiousity. One of the writers,

John by name, makes this clear and gives the reasons for the reports as 'that you might believe that Jesus is the Christ, the Son of God, and that believing you may have life in his name.'

That baby, born in a stable, grew in grace and truth and, in the fullness of his manhood started his work of redemption. He went to John, a Prophet, to be baptised and associate himself with the sinners of this world. He must have been very noticeable, however, as he was not blemished by sin. After rejecting the temptations of the Evil One to go on a path other than his Father had set, Jesus Christ began his ministry of teaching and healing.

Travelling around his little country Jesus showed by word and by action that he was both God and man. Even a cursory reading of the Gospel records allows no other reasonable explanation.

He was God in human form. As is only to be expected from the Son of God, his every action was guided by compassion and love. He seemed to burn with a divine love. He healed the sick, gave sight to the blind, gave hearing to the deaf, cured the leper and even raised the dead, alleviating earthlings from the curse of pain and sickness which afflicts this planet. The elements, such as the wind and the waves, obeyed him. With him all things were possible.

Also he was truly a man. He knew what it was to be tired, weary, thirsty, lonely, and fearful and he wept real tears of sorrow. Indeed, at the graveside of his friend, Lazarus he sobbed bitter tears even though he knew that with a word, which he would soon speak, he could restore his friend to life again. But he surely wept at the curse of death that plagued this planet. He was truly a very human man in every sense of the word.

At first he was very popular. Great crowds came to

hear his teaching and see his miracles. He spoke as no man had ever spoken before and taught the path of love and faith: love of God, the Creator of all things and love of one's neighbour, who was whoever was in need. He taught the need for faith, not only in the Father but in himself. Here he differed from all other teachers. He pointed people, not to the things he said, but to himself as the only way, the truth and the giver of life.

He offered rest and peace, and the way to know that was through repentance. From the beginning of his ministry this was his message - 'repent and believe'.

As the impact of his teaching reached the hearts of men and women, his popularity rapidly decreased. The children of the parents who had disobeyed the Creator in the garden of Creation at the beginning were still disobedient. Those in religious and political authority began to plot the death of this man from Nazareth. They recognised that he was calling for a new world with totally new human creatures where service was to be the highest achievement. All human standards were to be overturned. The greatest would be the humblest servant, every nobody would become a somebody and those who thought themselves somebody would be a nobody.

So evil hatred towards the Creator reached its peak in the way they treated the Prince of Glory. In a mockery of even this planet's justice, they arrested him. False evidence was laid against him, lying witnessess spoke against him, and the verdict was reached even before the trial. Those in authority were quite ruthless in the pursuit of this loving Jesus.

The Roman governor, representing the occupying power, hesitated when confronted by the dignity and essential majesty of the one we know as the Young Prince of Glory. But his mind was made up by the howling, hating mob. They did not want this man Jesus to reign over them. They wanted an earthly dictator rather than a heavenly King. How perverse these human creatures are! How can we ever understand them?

So they mocked, whipped and spat upon the gentle Jesus. Then they crucified him. This is one of the cruellest, most tortuous deaths that earthlings have ever devised. He was hung on a wooden cross, naked and shamed, tortured by nails and jeers. How can creatures act this way? It is shameful when they treat their own kind in such fashion but what happened that day was that the creatures were jubilantly killing their Creator. It can only be described as diabolical.

Adding to his sufferings must have been the fact that his own friends proved to be faithless - they ran away in fear when he was arrested. Only a few stood tearfully by the cross. That faithful band included his mother and one follower by the name of John. I found it difficult to read the Gospel record of this event, my eyes were continually being blinded with tears. How could such things be? It is beyond all comprehension!

Death is the end of all earthly stories. But it was not the end of this story. He came alive again. He rose immortalized and glorified. He who was alive and had been dead was now alive for ever more. The Creator God could never be defeated even when the forces of the Evil One and his earthly pawns were united in their wicked work. The Prince had been raised from the dead to take over the reins of authority in heaven and Earth. It must have been an awesome moment when he rose from the grave.

At first, his followers could not believe the news. Indeed, some refused to believe. But they found that it was true, empirically true. They saw him, ate with him, walked and talked with him. He showed his scarred hands and side. He showed them that he was the One foretold by the prophets of old, the promised One of whom the Good Book had spoken.

In this way salvation came to Earth, a way such as never could have been imagined. I had thought to my shame, dear Pzylon, that this planet must be beyond redemption but the loving Creator God found a way. His own Son paid the penalty for the sins of these human creatures and, through him and his finished work, the way has been made open for all to turn and come back to God. He offers forgiveness and acceptance and, by his Spirit makes even the most wicked into a new creature who will know his love and joy in their hearts.

Is all that not most wonderful? I can only stand in awe of such wisdom that made the evil acts of these earthlings into a vehicle for their salvation. From the death of the Prince he brought forth life, eternal life.

His followers, after being endowed with his Spirit, then went joyfully into all the world proclaiming the Good News of God. (I realise now that what makes so many of these earthlings doubly alien to me is that they do not, unless they belong to the Creator, bear within them his Holy Spirit. It all begins to fit into place!)

His followers had the exciting news that Jesus was alive and offered forgiveness and life to all who turned to him in simple trust. Although those followers met such opposition, even pain and death, they faithfully obeyed his call to go into all the world and preach the Good News to every human creature. And they found, as he had promised, that he was with them.

So Jesus, the Prince who is now King, is still active in this sad and strange place. He is still with his followers, calling men and women and even little children to come and follow him. In this part of the planet not many seem to hear or obey that call but some do leave the ways of death to accept his offer of life.

Beloved Pzylon, is not the story of the Prince on Earth a narrative worthy of the Creator himself? But it is a story not yet finished. He has promised to come back again to roll up the scroll of history. He will not return here in humility but in glory with all the holy angels with him. Then every knee shall bow and every tongue will confess that he alone is Lord.

It is a story of wonder upon wonder and the greatest wonder of all is that it is true! And the best is yet to be!

Greetings from a heart that is still warm with awe and wonder.

Repent and Believe

Greetings. I am glad you appreciated learning so much about the Prince's life here on this planet. Like you, I had but heard hints and echoes of his doings but never realised the full extent of his work. It truly is, as you suggested, an exciting and awesome story. The thoughts and ways of the Creator are far beyond our puny thinking and even our wildest imagination. All his works are well worthy of praise.

Worthy of praise throughout the whole universe but, sad to say, not among many in this place. Many earthlings have forgotten the doings of the Prince on Earth, or they ignore them. Even worse, many treat them as little more than tales to tell children to while away an idle hour or comfort them in the darkness of life. But what sort of imagination could dream up such a story? A story about the Son of God, vacating the glories and joys of heaven, emptying himself of such heavenly splendour and coming amongst earthlings as a mere man? Loving these hateful human creatures even to the extent of letting them kill him and, in dying, praying for their forgiveness? And in rising from the dead showing that his death is the gateway to eternal life! Such a story is surely beyond the devising of any human mind. Only the Great One, whose creative power is written in the stars and in the wonders of all creation, could conceive of such a plan!

Of course, as you and I know, Pzylon, it is no mere story but a real event, an actual historical occurence. It is true. Although it has the magical elements of a fairy tale it has the added marvel and miracle that it really happened 'once upon a time'.

Sadly, many do not believe and such people are completely beyond my comprehension. These humans, tainted by sin, often prefer the false comfort of lies to the invigorating challenge of truth. So they turn from the Creator and the truth that was personalised into this world and stumble blindly into the darkness. Jesus Christ, who was crucified by evil men, is still being crucified daily by many earthlings who mock him and use his name as nothing more than an idle oath.

Is it not incredible, beloved Pzylon, that these humans are offered forgiveness, and with forgiveness are bestowed love, joy and peace and yet they refuse? How can such things be?

As you can see I am torn by wonder at the Gospel Story and perplexed by the stupidity of these humans. But you have asked me what arrangements the Prince (who is now King here but of a rebellious Kingdom) has made for those who did not meet him in the flesh.

The first thing I must say is that he is still here on Earth, still walking these streets and byeways appealing to sinners to come and be healed. He is still offering forgiveness for the past, joy for the present and hope for the future. But he is no longer here in the flesh. His Spirit is still striving with all humans to come and follow him into the eternal Kingdom of his Father. He is present in his followers, witnessing through them and continuing his works of good to all in need.

It is amazingly simple how the Prince, who came to be Saviour to these humans, has made salvation available to them. He has made it a free gift. They do not need to buy forgiveness and acceptance with money or by works of charity or religion. That is perhaps why so many do not desire or comprehend it: consumerism is too deeply engrained into their lives to accept a gift which they cannot buy. They simply have to take the free offer which is made to them, the offer of eternal and happy life.

To accept this offer entails two things. They have to repent and believe.

Repentance means being sorry and doing something about it. It means reviewing one's life and recognizing that it has been one of failure. It requires acknowledging that they are not the sort of person they want to be, and more important, recognizing that they are not the sort of person whom God wants them to be. It is recognizing a need, and accepting the sad fact that they are helpless to improve themselves and live a life pleasing to God.

Being sorry for the sort of life he has been living is not enough for any earthling. Many are sorry and regretful but end up with nothing but being filled with self-pity. True repentance means throwing yourself helplessly on the Saviour and asking him for help. In a sense repenting means looking at one's self.

Believing means looking beyond one's self to the only one who can save - Jesus Christ. This faith is necessary for, as the Good Book has put it, 'without faith it is impossible to please God'. He delights when his human creatures turn to him in simple faith and trust, depending solely on him for their life here and the life to come. This seems so natural to us, dear Pzylon, but as my previous reports will have shown, this is not how humans usually act. This faith affects the whole being of the human creature.

It is a matter of the will. It is a deliberate act of refusing to trust idols of the earthlings' world, abandoning attempts at depending on one's own efforts, and trusting the Lord alone. Recognising that there is no-one else who can forgive and renew.

This means it is also a matter of the mind. These human creatures are not called to make some sort of leap into the unknown hoping to find eternal health and well-being. Rather it is a matter of examining the evidence for the Creator's work on Earth, through his Son, and assenting to its truth. It means reading or hearing the Good News as presented in the Good Book and recognising its truth. Those who do this find their hearts warmed.

So faith is also a matter of the heart. The heart of the human creature who believes finds its centre and base in the life, death and resurrection of the Lord Jesus. This, of course, has emotional consequences. How can it be otherwise when they find that the Creator of all things has loved them, even when they were enemies, and has done everything possible to bring them back to himself. The penalty for their sin has been taken on another's shoulders and the way is wide open for them to become children of God. If such thoughts do not move a human heart how hard that heart must be!

Faith affects will, mind and heart and this is then worked out in the body. Habits, actions and even the way things are done begin to change. They find a new law written in their hearts, not just commandments and precepts but the law of love. They are now new creatures doing new work.

Perhaps I have made this sound very complicated,

beloved Pzylon, but it is not so. I suspect many here make it even more complicated. But it really is as it was in the beginning when the Prince was on Earth and started to proclaim the Good News of God by saying 'Repent and Believe'. Many earthlings heard that call and responded just as today many still respond.

They find salvation which means being freed from the power and penalty of their sins and rebellion against the High and Holy One. Endless blessings attend this gift of salvation and I use the word 'endless' literally. This sad old Earth with its sorrows, pains, sins and deaths, which has troubled me so much, will pass away and there will be a new Heaven and a new Earth for the people of the Prince. Then the end results of that sacrifice on the cross by the Saviour will be seen in all their glory. It will indeed be a Kingdom such as this universe has never seen.

Meanwhile, sorrow, pain, sin and death have not departed from this Earth. In spite of the free offer of the Creator to these humans, many more ignore or refuse it. They live for the present, mock the idea of judgment and laugh at the idea of a hell where they must face a Godless and loveless eternity. I find this sort of attitude beyond my understanding. How can any creature act in this way? What a terrible place this is - they murdered the Son of God and treat his memory with disdain! Do you wonder that I do not like this place?

However, all is not lost. There are humans who hear the call of the Saviour, who do repent and believe and find new life in him. With some it is a sudden transformation, becoming new creatures almost instantaneously, whilst with others is seems to be part of a process. But it does happen. I have observed some of them. I must report on some of the ones I have seen. But not now.

I find myself in a strange dichotomy and worry - if such a thing is possible. When I consider the works of the Creator's hand I am consumed with wonder and praise. When I think of what he has done for these self-centred human creatures I am awestruck and amazed. Truly it is a love that is divine and beyond any creature's comprehension.

Then I look at these humans. They ignore the commands of the Creator, idly discard his offer of salvation, and apparently happily go on their way as if there will be no tomorrow. They eat and drink and try to forget they must die. They search for pleasure and satisfaction in the passing amusements of the day and disregard the endless joy on offer from the Eternal One. They long for life and take no notice of the One who came to give it - the Lifegiver himself. I weep and worry for these creatures, dear Pzylon.

However, the Creator has given them a choice so that they can crown the Prince or reject him. I tremble that so many of them want to reject him rather than kneel in humble adoration. This truly is a sad place.

I close now, worshipping and worrying. As always I send you my prayers for peace and harmony.

Boredom to Blessing

Shamar to Pzylon: Earth Report 24

Greetings. Some time ago, in an earlier report, perhaps one of the earliest, I revealed to you the story of a young human called Arthur. Knowing you, beloved Pzylon, you will readily recall that report. Would that I was as good at record-keeping!

Arthur is young, was unemployed and living a completely aimless life. He had withdrawn into himself, lost interest in everything and everyone and spent most of his waking hours lying on his bed listening to the music and inane chatter of his radio. I reported on him because he seemed to illustrate something of what is going on here in this sad place. Now all has changed for Arthur. The Prince has claimed Arthur as one of his followers! It has been a transforming experience, even a dramatic one.

It all began quietly, almost casually, with an apparently chance meeting. Arthur had been to the Youth Employment Office where he had been called to an interview. After waiting almost an hour in the office he had been seen by an official and instructed to go to a training centre for interview the next day. This depressed him intensely as he had become so used to his idle existence that the thought of daily work was almost frightening to him. But he knew he would have to go for the interview or he would lose his weekly allowance.

As he walked slowly homewards he met a young man he had known at school. 'Hullo Arthur,' was the greeting. 'How are you getting on? Still full of fun and games?'

Arthur stared at the boy, trying to recall his name and vaguely disturbed at the greeting. He could scarcely remember the time when he was full of 'fun and games.'

'You don't know me, do you?' laughed the young man. 'It's James - Jim Walters. Remember? Do you fancy going in for a cup of coffee and talking over old times?'

Arthur was confused. 'Coffee? I wouldn't mind a pint. Let's go to the pub.'

'Sorry, Arthur, I don't drink. I used to but I'm a Christian now. I gave it up.'

Without quite knowing how it had happened, Arthur found himself sitting in a little cafe, drinking coffee and listening to the bright and enthusiastic talk of Jim Walters. There was much laughter as they talked about some of the events of schooldays but Arthur was puzzled by his friend's claim that he was now a Christian. He had used it almost as a passing remark and had then continued to chat as a normal human being. Arthur had always thought of Christians as solemn, serious killjoys who were more interested in finding faults than in making pleasant conversation. Then it suddenly occured to him that he had never really met a Christian before. In a gap in the conversation, he said, 'What did you mean when you said you were a Christian?'

Jim told his story simply. As Arthur listened it almost seemed as if he was listening to an account of his own life.

'It was just over a year ago. I was living an aimless sort of life, one job after another but nothing lasting. I was really doing nothing and getting nowhere. I didn't even know what I wanted to do. Of course there was fun - drinking with the boys, chasing the girls but nothing really satisfying. It's a long story but I went to a youth rally in the church. I gave my life to Jesus that night, Arthur. It's great - really great. He's now my Saviour and Master. I'm living, well trying to live, for him. He gives real life.' Jim went on but Arthur was not listening to the words. It was Jim's enthusiasm that was communicating. Then he realised that Jim had asked a question and was awaiting an answer.

'What did you say?' he asked.

'Will you come to the rally tonight? I'll pick you up at 7 o'clock. I've a motorbike, you know.'

'Me at a church! No way!' said Arthur, suddenly afraid of what he was letting himself in for when making any sort of commitment.

On his way home Arthur had decided he would not go to the church rally that evening. There was no way he was going to become a religious maniac. Yet he was struck by the fact that, whatever could be said about Jim, he did not act like a religious maniac who wanted to do nothing but preach all the time. He almost felt guilty at the idea of letting Jim down by not going to the church rally.

With a roar of his motorbike Jim arrived for Arthur at exactly 7 o'clock. 'I'm not going,' said Arthur dogmatically.

'Come on, you'll enjoy it.' Jim had a persuasive tongue and Arthur found himself sitting on the pillion seat of the motorbike going to something he had never imagined possible - he was going to church.

He was surprised to find quite a number of young people in the church hall where the meeting was to be held. They were friendly and there seemed to be a lot of laughter which Arthur found, in his vague depression, rather disturbing. Then followed what was, for him, an hour of boredom and embarrassment. They sang hymns which he did not know, said prayers and read from the Bible. He did not know when to stand or sit or how to look up the Bible as the rest were doing. It was all alien to him so that he sat and wondered why he had come. Indeed several times he thought of walking out but was afraid they would shout at him and make him come back, showing him up in front of everyone.

Then the preacher started speaking. Arthur was not sure if he understood it all as the man spoke about the promise of Jesus to give life to all who came to him. But the man kept repeating the words,'I have come to give you life' and it was the word 'life' that kept reverberating through Arthur's mind. He began to think that although he had been alive all his life he had never really been more than merely existing. He had been what the preacher called 'going through the motions of life without actually being alive.'

Arthur felt he was beginning to understand vaguely what the preacher was saying when another topic was introduced. 'Sin is death,' announced the preacher and Arthur felt himself lost again. It seemed all too complicated to understand. But some things were getting through to his mind. Arthur began to realise that he had not lived for God, or indeed for anyone else, but had pursued a totally self-centred existence. He had always looked upon himself as number one and all things existed for his benefit.

At that meeting Arthur found himself doing something he had not done for years - thinking. Thinking about himself, his way of living, about God and the God-Man Jesus who came to give life. But his thoughts were all confused. It would be mad to become a Christian - everyone would laugh at him. It would be mad not to become a Christian and taste real life for a change. He reflected that these young people, like Jim, certainly seemed alive. Compared with them he was just a member of the walking dead.

At the end of the rally the preacher made an appeal for those who wanted to give themselves to Christ to come forward. Arthur wanted to walk forward and, at the same time, was ashamed of such a thought. He would make a spectacle of himself by walking to the front of the church hall. Even while his mind was debating whether to go forward or not he found himself walking to the front.

That night Arthur bowed the knee to the Prince and confessed that Jesus Christ is Lord. He was a confused, bewildered penitent with a simple, yearning faith, but the Lord accepted him and gave him new life.

So Arthur is now a follower of the Prince. He has not found it easy, for his parents and sister greeted the news with laughter. But the church has become a home and family to him. He is now training to be a painter, and, to his surprise, finding he likes the job. Reading the Bible and praying now seem second nature to him and he is finding life to be more of an exciting venture rather than a boring existence. He is a changed man.

Such things warm my heart and lift my spirit, Pzylon. Arthur has caught a glimpse of the blessings I wish you - peace and harmony.

Church and Christians

Shamar to Pzylon: Earth Report 25

Greetings and again apologies. I do know I should have reported on the Church here in this place but became sidetracked. It is very easy to get distracted in this place and as you know, beloved Pzylon, I am not an organised thinker. This is such a strange and sad place that it is a delight to have good news to report, which is why I sent the account of Arthur being claimed by the Prince.

That is enough about my 'wayward reporting' as you call it. Let me turn to the questions you raise about the followers of the Prince and their ways of gathering together in communities of believers.

When the Prince was here he founded his Church which would eternally triumph even over death and hell itself. They would be a people who would serve and praise him, worshipping and witnessing to his grace and the love of the Father. It would be a glorious company united in faith, hope and love.

As the Good Book says, 'Christ loved the Church and gave his life for her.' So, in the eyes of the Creator and his Son, the Church is a precious inheritance, called and kept by the Spirit of God himself. It is indeed the family of God, his children, his flock, a holy nation, a royal priesthood, called from the darkness of this world into his glorious light to show forth his praises. Reading through the words of the New Testament in the Good

Book it is almost as if there are not enough adjectives, or images, to describe fully the Church of Jesus Christ.

Considering that it started with a pitifully small band of humans, it is astonishing that it is now a great worldwide company. Indeed, it is now to be found in almost every nation, tribe and tongue. A glorious worldwide company.

Sadly, and perhaps not unexpectedly in this fallen world, the worldwide Church is not a united body. It is tragic to see a divided Church in a divided world, but it is a fact. The sin which infects all things here has corrupted even the Church of God so that differences in doctrine and emphasis have brought about divisions in the Church.

In spite of this, the Lord knows all those who are his and they are united in Christ Jesus and, although they belong to different branches of the earthly Church, they are true members of the great universal Church which the Prince is building.

But my task is not to report on worldwide affairs but to observe this particular part of the planet. So I will concentrate on what I have seen here in this place. That means I will simply report on the local churches.

In every city, town and village here there are churches. In common language the word 'church' usually refers to the building, not to the people who gather there. I should say a word about these buildings. Some are splendid in scope and intention with tall spires pointing to the heavens, great vaulted roofs that seem to dwarf mere humans before the presence of God, and stained glass windows with glowing colours illustrating biblical scenes. Other churches are small and unadorned, simply meeting places. Whatever the architectural design the church building, it seems to me, should be a witness to the Creator and what goes on inside.

But many of the church buildings I have seen here in this sector of the planet seem to shame the Creator who has made so much loveliness all around. Some are drab, ugly, unkept and obviously neglected as to their appearance. I find it sad that so many meeting places of the Prince's people are so dull and dreary-looking. Is not the Lord of the Church the One who has scattered beauty all around his creation?

However, as I have said, the Church is people not buildings. The Prince did not promise to create buildings that would stand against all the forces of hell.

Dear Pzylon, I began this report with the intention of being positive rather than negative in all that I record. I am fully aware of the many times you have accused me of 'looking on the black side' and being 'pessimistic' in all my interpretations. Sorry, I am already reporting my criticisms about church buildings and emphasising the things that shocked or troubled me. So, in considering the people who meet in these buildings I now promise to look on the bright side! I will say nothing about hypocrites, false teachers, churches which seem to be more social clubs than worshipping communities or so-called leaders and members who really bring shame on the name of the Prince. These, sadly, can almost be taken for granted in this sad place.

The glorious truth is that the Prince has his people here. Some congregations (those who meet in church buildings) are much larger than others, but I do not think numbers are a measure of success. Apparently the Prince did not think so either. He promised that where two or three are gathered together in his name he would be there with them. Such words are rather touching as they show his love for individuals rather than vague masses of humans.

In an age of disbelief many local Churches are blessed with faithful teachers. These have many names according to what part of the Christian tradition they belong; ministers, vicars, pastors, elders and so on. They faithfully proclaim the Word of God and seek to build up the faith of the people whom they are called to lead. Many could have successful careers in the affairs of this Earth, earning high salaries and prestige, but they are content to serve their Master by being a shepherd of the flock. I can only salute such men who obeyed the call of the Prince to educate and guide the people of God in dark and difficult days. They have great responsibilities and will have great reward when the Prince comes as King to reign in glory.

Then there are many humble members of the Church who have become burdened with sin and failure and have cast their burden upon the Lord. Week by week they gather to worship him, sing his praises, listen to his Word and seek his strength for the days ahead. They delight to walk in the pathways of their God, trying to reflect his love, and be purifiers and illuminators in a corrupt and dark age. They struggle not to conform to the false standards of this world but seek to have their minds renewed by the Spirit of all truth. I can only honour such human creatures. It is comforting to know that the Creator has his own people here and is not ashamed to own them as his own sons and daughters.

By bowing their knee to the Prince, and confessing that he alone is Saviour, they have handed their lives over to his hands. By losing their own sinful lives they have discovered true life - a joyous life.

Such Churches, with such people, are a true family

belonging to one another, weeping with those who weep and rejoicing with those who rejoice. They care for one another, support one another and their love for one another spills over into the community. I have observed such Christians being hospitable to one another, but more than that, visiting the sick and doing little tasks for their neighbours - even though the neighbours do not believe. This world is not worthy of such saints or such saintly actions.

Indeed, I do not think earthlings recognise how much they owe to the Church, either universally or locally. Many of the social benefits and communal care which they enjoy started with the Church putting the love of God into action. The Christians founded hospitals to care for the sick and hospices to surround the dying with love. They fought to banish slavery and battled for each individual to be treated aright. Missionaries travelled far, not only taking the Good News of God but medical care and education to those who knew nothing of such things. I fear it would be an even more terrifying world but for the Church and all her works.

Then at a local level Churches still do an amazing amount of work for the good of the community. Often they are the ones who care for the destitute, the homeless and the addict. Recently, in this sector of the planet, much publicity was given to some pop singers for raising millions of pounds for the famine areas of the world. But there is little publicity for these Christians who, year by year, are giving millions for a needy world.

Most local Churches have Sunday schools for children and various youth organisations. Their hope is that these young humans will grow up in the faith and serve the Prince all the days of their lives. This hope is not always fulfilled. But this can be said - even where the Church fails to win them for her Lord they have instilled some moral values into these young humans. At least many turn out to be good citizens. I am not sure if the world recognises this fact. Certainly the Church receives little public honour for her works. Of course, the Prince who founded the Church was crucified by this world and servants cannot be expected to be treated differently from their Master.

One thing has now struck me, Pzylon. This world, as I have reported, is a bad place. But what would it have been like if there had been no Church working to bring the love of God into the dark planet?

The existence of the Church here in this place has brought comfort to my heart. It is not perfect - nothing here is - but it does reflect something of the sort of community that the Creator must have meant this world to be. A place where people are happy together and there are no social, cultural or racial barriers - they simply love their God and their neighbour. In two words - peace and harmony in all that they do.

I wish you that peace and harmony.

Offer of Life

Greetings from this planet of rebellion. I must confess that I still waver between joy and despair as I observe these human creatures. Although I know the Creator has a great love for them and that the Prince has come to open the way for them to recover all, and indeed more, than they lost in the intended paradise, they still act as if they were alone in the universe. They seem to assume that they are able to solve all problems by their own strength and wisdom. I find such an attitude infinitely sad.

Occasionally, however, I find signs of hope. I reported on the surprising conversion of Arthur, the boy who moved from boredom to blessings. This is not always the way the Prince works in calling humans to life. He was a friend of fishermen while here on Earth and sometimes uses their tactics in pulling some human creatures to himself. He gets a hook into them, playing with them so that their struggles only ensure that the victory will be his - of course, he is pulling them to life, not death. I wonder if he is doing that with the Callington family.

You will remember that I reported on the Callington family as an example of those who have everything and yet nothing. They have many of the riches of this world but, as a family, they are in danger of falling apart. The husband is worried about losing his job, his wife is

151

being tempted to ignore her marriage vows, the son is already experimenting with drugs, and Pamela, the daughter, fears she is pregnant.

I feared for the future of that family but now I see a glimmer of hope. There is no great change in their circumstances but I suspect the Prince, as a fisher of souls, has his hook into the family through Pamela.

It came about this way. Pamela discovered that her fears of being pregnant were false. That morning she walked through the village feeling a warm glow of relief and happiness in her whole being. Feeling rather childish she wanted to run and skip and shout her news to all the world. One of the great tragedies of these humans is that, when they are joyful or thankful, they have no one to thank - they have forgotten their Creator!

As Pamela passed by the village church she noticed it was open. Without thinking she went into that little church and, as she entered, realised she had never been in it before. There was an air of peace and tranquility in the shadowy building which turned her joy to solemnity. She found herself sitting on a hard pew staring with unseeing eyes at the table in front with a silver cross and two unlit candles. Suddenly it all became blurred as tears flooded into her eyes. She had no thoughts, no words, only tears streaming down her cheeks. She did not know whether she was weeping because of relief or loneliness or for a vanishing innocence. She suddenly felt unclean.

"Can I help you, dear?" An elderly woman, slipped into the pew beside Pamela. Throwing a duster over the seat in front she embraced Pamela, cuddling her head against her apron-covered breast. Almost with childlike relief Pamela sobbed into the soft breast of the old woman, vaguely aware of hands caressing her hair and soft words of comfort being spoken.

"I don't know why I'm crying," said Pamela, her sobs dying away.

"It does us all good to get a good cry now and again. Do you want to tell me all about it?"

"No," wailed Pamela, and then suddenly found herself pouring it all out into the woman's sympathetic ear. As she finished her story, realizing how sordid it really was, she ended, "I suppose I've been a bad girl."

"There are none of us good, dear. None of us good," sighed the old woman. "But he knows all about it. He'll keep you if you want."

"Who knows?" asked Pamela in sudden panic. She had not even told the stable boy.

"The Lord, of course," answered the old woman. "You've come to the right place. Just tell him it all. Say you are sorry. He will forgive and help you. I know."

They sat talking for a long while together in that little village church. It ended with Pamela helping the old woman to clean the church, dusting and polishing happily, something she had never done at home. When they parted, Pamela promised to meet the old woman at the church door the next day and to go to the morning service.

The future is not mine to see, as you know, Pzylon, but I have hopes that Pamela is setting off towards the path of life. If she does, perhaps she can be the means of showing her father that life is more than work and ambition, be an example to her mother that joy is to be found in serving the Prince and help her brother to realise that true life is not to be found in chemically altering the molecules of the mind. I do not know and can only hope.

So many of these human creatures reject or scoff at the

offer of life. The Evil One seems to have a fierce grip on their hearts and minds. How can we understand such things? Is it not truly beyond all comprehension? The Creator offers them a new creation, life instead of death, joy instead of despair, forgiveness instead of guilt and the assurance of living happily evermore. Yet they reject it!

I witnessed one sad incident which illustrates the ignorance of this world. On a bus a little girl sat at the window looking out. As the bus passed an imposing building the little girl asked her mother,

"Mummy, what's that place?" The mother glanced outside and said, "It's a church." The girl looked up at her mother and asked, "What's a church?" There was a few moments silence before the mother spoke, almost angrily, "Stop asking questions and sit up straight."

Suddenly, and sadly, I realised why the woman did not answer her daughter's question. How could she say that a church is a building where people to go to acknowledge and worship the great Creator who made them, loved them, and wants only the best for his creatures? How could she say that it is the place where people go to sing praises to God, listen to his words of wisdom, ask for help for daily living and seek forgiveness for their sins? How could she say any of these things when she knew the next question - 'Why don't we go?'

In spite of the good, this is a depressing place to such as I who know the goodness of the Creator.

But I wish you peace and harmony.

Request to Leave

Greetings and a request. I formally seek permision to leave this place and return home. This, I must point out, is not the result of the mood of the moment but something I have seriously and carefully considered. Please give it your immediate attention.

There are two reasons for this request. Firstly, I am aware of how I have failed and, secondly, I am assailed with a soul sickness for the peace and harmony of my own homeland.

I am very conscious of how much I have failed. I came to this place of glory and horror with an organised plan to observe in a logical sequence many facets in the life of these human creatures. That plan fled my mind when I found myself confronted by the reality of life in a world in rebellion against its Creator, indeed a world apparently at war with itself. The confusion which this aroused in my mind certainly affected my reporting, as you know. I found myself taking up one thing after another without really following up anything in any depth or sensible sequence. Your criticism in this respect was justified. So many things seemed to demand my attention that I forgot the plan and reported on the events and stories of the moment. Truth to tell, I found I could do no other.

I can only ask your forgiveness, beloved Pzylon, for the confusion in my mind and in the order of my reporting. Also, I need your pardon for the elements of self-pity which kept invading my observations. May I receive that forgiveness and pardon personally? I do wish to return.

Then I have failed in my mission by the many areas of human life on which I have not reported. There are so many aspects of life on this planet which I seem to have ignored completely, and many others that I have done little more than mention. Many of these are important and influential in the daily living of these human creatures.

I have reported nothing on education systems, politics, economics, governments and patterns of civic authorities. From what I remember, I think I have only mentioned science and technology in passing, ignoring the way in which they can be a blessing and a curse. There can be no doubt that science has given increased wealth, welfare and comfort to those humans. Medical science has indeed abolished many diseases and alleviated many pains. But it has also brought terrifying instruments of power and manipulation which is not for the good.

Then there is the whole pop culture in this place which is worthy of many reports and yet I have practically ignored it. Young humans are treated as almost a separate species with their own music and lifestyle. The list of the areas which I have covered could be extended almost endlessly. There are nations and races; wars; terrorism; industrialisation and ideas of progress; inhuman cities and crime - all these and more are areas I should have observed and reported on. But I did not. My failures are many and I fear that I have proved myself unworthy of the task that was given to me.

Allied to this awareness of failure is the true fact

that I am, in a word, homesick. As I have reported times beyond number, I do not like this place. It's values are not our values, its standards are not our standards and there seems little here of the peace and harmony that dwells in my own heart. The sickness of sin means that the kindest human can be cruel and the cruellest kind. At times it seems to me that all earthling things are perverted.

They largely ignore the Creator. This really is beyond my understanding. The wisest of men, in philosophy and science, boast of how they seek to discover the truth behind all things. They claim to have an open mind to find this truth then they close their minds to the basic fact of a Creator! Is this not strange?

I do not like Earth but - there must be a but! - It really is a world of astonishing beauty and awesome grandeur. The Creator did not make a planet of necessities for his creatures - he showered loveliness all around. Here there are so many brilliantly coloured flowers, ever-changing landscapes, shining rivers, graceful birds, delightful animals in this fair and pleasing world. Why is so much of it being spoiled by the thoughtless actions of these human creatures? But they cannot take away the glory that is built into the creation, neither the sweetness of the flowers nor the beauty of the rainbow.

I believe that only those who know the Creator can appreciate the creation. Certainly those who have bowed the knee to the Young Prince of Glory, the Lord Jesus Christ, can fully enjoy all the gifts of their God.

This is the root problem of this planet. It is a good world, a very good world but it has been, and is being, spoiled not only in the ecological balance of nature, but in the human heart: a heart that is self-willed and self-centred and can only lead to destruction, not only of all around, but of itself.

As I have reported, the Creator has made provision for these human creatures to start afresh, to become new creatures in Christ Jesus, and begin the work of the new creation. But, tragically, there are earthlings who do not take up this offer of salvation.

What a sad and bewildering place Earth is! Can I be blamed for not liking it? It is a good world spoiled.

So, Pzylon, this is the reason for my homesickness. I yearn with a great longing for a good world - my own. I ache to be back in the realms of untarnished beauty, where love to the Creator alone governs all actions, and peace and harmony pervade all things. I want to be back where there is continuous rejoicing in all the gifts of the Creator and where there is no pain, sin or the curse of death. Indeed, I hunger and thirst to be home with all that that means. Home where I can be myself and yet live for others, where I can be an individual and yet glory in the fact that I belong to a community. I simply want to be in a realm where there is no sin, hate, or fear.

Perhaps only those who have lived here on this planet can fully appreciate the depth of my longing. There is so much pain here, even for the innocent.

Yesterday I saw a man, painfully hobbling along on crutches, following the hearse containing the coffins of his dead wife and baby daughter. Only a week before they had been going home after visiting the grandmother of the child. Standing at the roadside waiting to cross, a car had ploughed into them, killing mother and child and leaving the husband injured. It had been a young driver, drunk, out for a joy-ride in a stolen car.

Such scenes must forever stay in my mind. How can it be otherwise? Then I saw an old woman being led into a nursing home. Her face was stern and she held back the tears as she tried to retain her dignity. But she was old and frail, unable to look after herself, and her sons and daughters did not want to take on the responsibility. I can only wonder if such things are right!

I observed a little boy sitting on a doorstep waiting for his mother to come home from her work. He had been sent home early from school and could not get into his own home.

I saw a woman with powder on her face as a disguise for the black eye her husband had given her. She had got used to the beatings.

Forgive me, beloved Pzylon, but even this, hopefully my last report, is wandering around all sorts of subjects and events. The pain of these people keeps crashing into my mind and sensitivities. I do not like it here.

So, again, can I repeat my formal request to leave this sad place and return home, either to abandon my mission or simply to return for a brief respite from the strange and sad place? Perhaps, after a rest in my own realms of glory, I could return to complete my task.

I am in your hands. Meanwhile I wish you that which I find hard to retain here - peace and harmony.

Postscript

For some time now there have been no more reports from Shamar and I can only assume that he has received permission to leave this 'sad and strange place' as he called it. Whether he has gone forever or will return after the requested rest, I cannot say.

I miss his observations and insights and can only hope that he is recovering from the pains and sorrows we apparently inflicted on him. It is not difficult to understand his longing to leave our troubled and fallen world and be in the realms of love, peace and harmony. He has left a longing in my own heart for such a world. Or perhaps it has always been in my heart and he has brought it into my mind. Surely the world, and human life, was not meant to be as it is?

J.W.